Julie's Star

Julie's Star

SHOOTING STAR SERIES BOOK 1

LESLEY ESPOSITO

authorHOUSE®

AuthorHouse™
1663 Liberty Drive
Bloomington, IN 47403
www.authorhouse.com
Phone: 1-800-839-8640

Published by AuthorHouse   11/08/2012

ISBN: 978-1-4772-8538-1 (sc)
ISBN: 978-1-4772-8537-4 (e)

Library of Congress Control Number: 2012920273

Chapter 1

The after work and before dinner rush was clearing out of the supermarket. That is how it is in the north end of Manhattan. It is mostly a residential area. The masses get off the subways and hit the supermarket to carry home what they can and then cook dinner. Molly reached down to grab the paper towels to wipe down and clean the little conveyor belt that moved the foods along to the register. She heard whining and thought there was some sort of electrical issue but then realized it was a female voice. The women was obviously in a rush and had no patience. She was probably used to being waited on, Molly grumbled to herself.

"Hello, where is the cashier, I'm running late and I need to get out of here!"

Molly kept herself down for a few more seconds just for fun. She was able to peek up to see the woman with the high pitch whine. She was not by herself though. The couple seemed to be right out of the social section. She was tall and slim with short blonde hair and dressed as if just out of the latest Vogue magazine. He stood just above the woman and had dark brown hair with an athletic build but not body builder big. He looked right out of GQ magazine. A perfect compliment to each other. Except he seemed somewhat aloof and unaware of the woman he was with. Molly generally did not judge people but after many years at this job she was fairly observant and learned to read people. There was definitely something not right with this couple.

Molly suspected they were going to a dinner party in the area. Judging from the items on the conveyor they probably did not like them too much. Cheap chocolate and wine. If they could afford those clothes they could do a little better. Well who was she to judge. She just had a tendency to make up stories about people's lives. It helped to pass the time.

When Molly finally got up she stumbled and in slow motion she saw the spray bottle go tumbling onto the conveyor and as her luck would have it the trigger hit hard spraying at the couple standing in her line. Of course in all her time at this job this had never happened and it would happen when the couple of perfection was standing there. And of course the bottle was set to full force stream. The spray had hit the the man on his shirt. Well at least it didn't go below his belt.

"Oh shit, I'm so sorry, here are some paper towels," she handed over the roll.

"It's ok, really no big deal it will dry as soon as we step back outside." He turned back to his girlfriend, "I don't know why you made me wear long pants and a long sleeve shirt. It's stifling hot out tonight."

"You look great honey," the blonde woman said as she trailed a finger down his chest showing her brilliant white teeth. "Besides our outfits compliment each other and we look great together." But then she turned at sneered at Molly, "except for the wet spots."

"I said I was sorry."

"I would rather be wearing shorts and flip flops."

"Darling this is a dinner party not a beach party."

Molly thought she heard him grumble something about them never attending a beach party. He looked defeated as he slid his hands in his pocket.

Blondie did hear how he responded, "you know sand does not agree with me dear." But she said it through gritted teeth, obviously the conversation was over.

Molly had heard these types of conversations so many times over the years so she was not paying too much attention. She rang up the purchases and moved to the bagging area. She took another look at this poor sap. While he looked annoyed he still stood tall and confident. She did not pay much attention to men in general but she could appreciate a good looking man when she saw one. And he was definitely good looking.

She very rarely interjected on conversations and was surprised when she heard herself say, "well I think you would look good in anything." Or even nothing she added in her head.

He looked at her, staring straight into her eyes, "are you flirting with me?"

She felt like his eyes were boring into her secret thoughts. She was a little embarrassed especially since she was picturing strong arms and a bare broad chest. She blushed and turned and said, "I was just making an observation."

Blondie suddenly realized what was going on and shot ice cold daggers at Molly. Wow she was scary Molly thought. All right time to get them out of here.

"You both look great really, that will be $28.35."

The boyfriend pulled out his debit card to finish the transaction when blondie asked where they could buy some flowers. The florist was not very close by so she directed them to the pre wrapped bouquets in the corner of the store.

Blondie sighed and said, "ok that will have to do, I will be right back" and trotted off to grab the flowers.

"She is not so bad."

Molly shrugged her shoulders, "it is really none of my business."

"She means well. She is in the fashion industry so she is always up on the latest trends and making sure I dress for the occasion."

"You don't have to explain." She wished they would just hurry up and leave. This was getting uncomfortable for her. Conversation with men were not her strong point, especially with good looking confident types even if he was controlled by his girlfriend.

Jason had to step aside as there were other customers coming onto the line. The longer Anna took to get the flowers the longer he watched this curious woman at the register. She was so different than Anna and he could not take his eyes off her. She had luxurious black hair that fell to her shoulders. Deep green eyes and soft pale skin with perfectly placed freckles. It was such an odd combination. And her eyes showed intelligence beyond this job. But there was also a shyness, intrigue and an inner flirtatiousness that she obviously did not show very often. He wondered so many things about her. What nationality were her parents that gave her that exotic look. Why this job and not something else? What she looked like in a dress, in nothing. He stopped himself there. He had a girlfriend and should not let his mind wander like this. Luckily Anna returned and they had to get behind several others.

He turned to his girlfriend. There was something they had not settled yet. "Have you decided to go to St. Lucia with me yet?"

"I told you I don't do Caribbean especially not in the summer. Why would I go from one hot place to another?"

"And I told you that I needed a work break and I got a good deal. Besides I thought you were between major shoots."

She sighed at him. "How about Europe? Tuscany would be so romantic, great food and wine."

"Or do you mean shopping in Rome and Milan?" He may not have the great fashion sense she did but he knew where the major shopping capitals in the world were. And he knew Anna. "Besides we just went to Paris."

Molly was trying hard to ignore the couple but as they moved up in the line it was hard not to overhear. She could not believe the selfishness of that woman. She still was not sure what was overcoming her today. Maybe it was the years of working and just making it in this city with little left over to do much of anything, she was proud of her accomplishments but this was too much to bear.

Molly glared at the women, "I can't believe you won't go to the Caribbean just because it is summer."

"Not that it is any of your business but not only is it passé . . ."

Molly was only half listening to her list of reasons not to go. She was interested in the boyfriends reaction. He looked frustrated, tense. She tried to convince herself she did not care but when their eyes met there was an odd connection. One that said they understood each other. Molly looked away feeling flushed, a feeling she was not used to. Realizing the women finally stopped carrying on she commented, "you are lucky your boyfriend takes you all over the world. Some people never get to go anywhere, if someone offered me the chance to go to the Caribbean I would take it in a heartbeat."

The women rolled her eyes, "whatever," and shrugged off the conversation. They finished the transaction and she took her flowers. "Come on Jason we are running late." She grabbed his arm and headed towards the door.

So that was his name, not that she cared Molly reminded herself. But it was a nice name, it seemed to suit him. Whoever he was. She wondered what he did that they could go to Paris and the tropics. How long had they been together and why did he stay with her.

She watched them head to the door and saw Jason turn and look back at her one last time. He held her gaze for a few seconds. He hesitated as if he was going to say something but he was being dragged towards the door. The contact was broken and Molly was breathing again.

Jason had a sudden thought which caused him to turn back to her. But it was such an absurd idea that he hesitated just enough that he realized they made it to the door. When he opened it for Anna there was such an onslaught of rain and wind that it actually pushed them back into the store.

"Ugh why can't we get out of this hell hole. Jason go grab us a cab."

"I'm not going out there, it should pass in a minute you know how these summer storms are."

"Another reason not to go to St. Lucia: hurricanes."

Jason grabbed his girlfriend's hand and marched up to the cashier. Molly was just as ready for them to leave the store as this woman. Then they were approaching her again. What did they forget now? It did not seem likely they wanted an umbrella. There was no way a drop of rain had ever touched that woman. But Jason kept his eye on her while pulling his girlfriend along. He did not seem interested in another purchase so she wondered what his sudden intensity was about.

He was a little nervous about what he was going to say but this topic was frustrating him, he needed to give Anna a jolt, try something drastic to get her on board. "Hi, my name is Jason and this is Anna and you are?"

"Molly," she answered with arms crossed over her chest.

"Well Molly, since my girlfriend here does not want to come on vacation with me, why don't you come instead?"

Both woman said "what!" simultaneously.

Molly was expecting to offer an opinion, not being asked on a trip, with a man she did not know. This was crazy, what was he thinking? She stood waiting for him to retract what he just said.

"Oh this is just great, because I won't go you are going to take some random stranger with you?"

"Well I have two plane tickets and an all inclusive package for two so I need to take someone with me."

"The cashier?" she questioned and looked at Molly with icy eyes, "that is who you would pick?"

"There is nothing wrong with being a cashier," Jason said in Molly's defense.

"For some under motivated people. Sure why not take her and you will see what you are missing, then we can jet off to Tuscany."

This was not quite the response he expected but somewhere deep in the back of his mind perhaps it was the one he wanted. Another chance to see this Molly again. He loved that name. He knew this was crazy. First he wanted to do this to convince Anna to come but now he wanted to do anything to get Molly to come.

He turned back to Molly with a new sparkle in his eye, "what do you say Molly, do you want to go to St. Lucia with me? You said you would jump at the chance."

Molly knew that St. Lucia was in the Caribbean but otherwise did not know much else about it. Not that it mattered, anywhere other than this island would be exotic to her. Travel was in her future goals but she was not one to read the travel section. Not just yet, she did not want to be distracted when she was so close to accomplishing her goal. But what was one week, what could it hurt? Her friend Katie was always telling her to get out more, well this was certainly getting out. But with someone she did not know? Maybe she would say yes just to piss off Anna. Who was she to judge her anyway? Just a cashier, what did she know? Well admittedly she had been judging her from the first time she heard her.

"You know what? Sure absolutely, I will go with you," she gave Jason her best smile and added, "'and I promise I will be great company."

This earned her another icy stare from Anna but Molly did not flinch and held her gaze right back. "You have no idea what Jason needs and you can't possible have anything for him," her eyes softened as she turned to Jason, "and darling when you are over this little game of yours I will give you what you need in Italy. I will start planning."

Was this woman defending him, he could not think of why. He seemed sure she was interested in him but so were a lot of women. It never affected him before but admittedly he was enjoying these two women having a little bantering over him. "Ok it's settled then, Molly you and I are going to St. Lucia."

Anna rolled her eyes again dragging Jason away, "let's go, we will be lucky if we make it for dessert at this point.

Jason turned back, "I'll be in touch."

Molly was sure that would be the last she would see of them. She was sure he was just using her to get to his girlfriend. Probably. But there was definitely a side of her that hoped this trip would happen.

Saturday morning coffee had been a ritual between Molly and Katie for a long time. Sometimes they would go to the local diner or to the coffee shop. Other times they would go to each others apartments but they always made a point to get together. It was one of the few times Molly had no school or work and it was before Katie's shift at the hospital. Katie was a pediatric nurse at the hospital and worked mostly evening shifts so this was their one time to catch up.

They had been friends since middle school but acted more like sisters. Molly often wished they were sisters but as much as she loved that family it was a little too crazy for her. Katie had four very protective brothers and their household was always on the border of chaos. It was great fun but Molly could not live like that all the time. Katie and her family had been a life saver for her so many times.

Molly had not slept well that night. She kept replaying the previous evening events over and over in her mind. She was trying to decide if Jason was sincere or just playing a cruel joke on her. She kept trying to let it go. Nothing was going to come of it but she felt sure there was some kind of weird connection between them.

Because of that she was a little slow moving so she had Katie come over to her place and even asked her to pick up the coffees on her way over. Katie just figured she was not feeling well but she was shocked when Molly told her about the trip. "And you actually agreed?" Once again Katie was very concerned for her friend.

"It was that blonde bitch, Katie, she was getting on my nerves. She was such a snob." Molly was getting tense from the memory of her icy glares.

"I can't hardly get you to go out on a Friday night and you agreed to a trip with someone you don't know."

Molly knew Katie was getting upset. She was right. For years she kept bugging Molly to go out, socialize, meet some people. Molly had been too focused on finishing school but she was right it was time to have some fun. But it was probably more about the fact that she did not know Jason. Who he was, where he lived? He did not seem to be some weird psycho since he had a girlfriend like Anna. So why did she agree she asked herself for the thousandth time.

Molly tried to put in words what she felt when he looked at her last night. "I know I don't know him but when he looked at me there was something more. Plenty of guys look at me, I know that, but it was like he was looking into to my soul, searching, trying to find the real me. I never felt like that before." She knew she sounded crazy. She shrugged and smiled, "or maybe I had something stuck in my teeth, dripping out my nose. So maybe he felt bad for me." She was still trying not to be overly optimistic. "Or maybe it was some crazy practical joke they play everywhere they go and were laughing their asses off as they left."

"Well if that is true I will personally hunt them down and give them a piece of my mind."

Molly smiled at that because she knew it was true. Once Katie decided something there was no stopping her. At least she had not threatened to put her brothers on them, she would have to bail someone out of jail for sure. That was also why she loved Katie's family so much, she knew they would always be there for her.

Molly drifted off a little remembering the dark eyes and the way they went from frustrated to intense to sparkling when she agreed to go with him. For the brief time they met, he made her feel like she mattered and that she was important. She knew it was crazy but at least she knew there was someone out there that could make her feel that way and she could think about finding someone for her.

"Oh I see," Katie interrupted her reminiscing, "so how good looking is this guy?"

Molly blushed at that. She had so little experience with men. She had not dated in years and she never talked about any man. She had to admit that he was very good looking. She smiled at Katie, "yeah there's definitely an attraction there."

"So let's just say he does come back, when is this trip, can you go, where is this island, do you even have a passport?"

Molly hesitated to admit that she had no other details. "I do have a passport, it's in the Caribbean and well I am not sure when it is, we did not get far."

Katie grabbed Molly's laptop and Googled St. Lucia. "Let's see French West Indies. Wow, very lush mountains and gorgeous beaches. Well at least he has good taste."

Molly closed her eyes and imagined herself sitting on the beach amongst the swaying coconut palms, tropical drink in hand. Maybe she will go with Jason but she decided just then that no matter what she would go someday, some way, some how.

Katie pulled her back out of her daydream yet again. "So how do you have a passport, you have never been anywhere."

"I thought about doing a college exchange program for a while but it did not work out, in any case it works for a photo I.D. since I don't have a drivers license."

"Always so practical. And what about flying?"

"Well, that makes me a bit nervous, I like to keep my feet on the ground. Who knows maybe I will like it. I think it would be worth it. Golden sunsets, blue waters," the images kept popping in her head. "Anyway you are always trying to get me out of the house. And now I'm trying to do something with myself and you are trying stop me."

"No I'm trying to make sure you don't run off with some psycho and then I will have to hunt him down, kill him and then I will go to jail."

"I know, trust me it has crossed my mind so many times. Like I said I will probably never see him again and I can just go back to my daydreams."

"Ok, promise if he does come back you will go out with him first, make sure he's not a psycho."

"Or plain ass weird."

"Drooler."

"Straw slurper."

"Spaghetti sucker."

They both broke down laughing but it was getting late and Katie got up to put her mug in the sink. "Ok, keep me posted I am off to work."

"Ok, love you talk to you later."

Later that day and downtown two men were having a late lunch in a private club. A trail of smoke floated in front of Jason. He could not find the pleasure in cigar smoking but his long time best friend liked it and there were no rules in private clubs about smoking. They had been coming here after becoming official members when they were twenty one. Both of their fathers were members and they continued the tradition. Outsiders were not often let in. Many business deals were made here, careers could be made or broken within these walls. Jason thought it was an honor to be a member even though it was more of an inheritance in a way. Still you could easily be kicked out. He did not like everyone or everything that went on here but it was good business, good social time and a place he could get away.

The man sitting across from him in the matching dark leather club chair was his long time friend Lewis. They grew up together, went to the same schools and business school. But while they grew up in the same circles, they were quite a bit different. Lewis was a bit more of a player and he was a more hardcore business man. They had an informal club within the club for future business rulers of the world as Lewis liked to call it. Jason wanted to be good, great at his job but he did not want to rule the world or even the country. Lewis on the other had definitely wanted that title. And that did not mean to be president of the country, it meant ruler of the financial world which in his mind was even more powerful than the president.

Lewis looked at Jason with a wicked grin, "that's quite a story my brother. What possessed you to invite a complete stranger, a cashier, on a trip with you?"

Jason was getting a little annoyed with the whole cashier thing. He tried not to be judgmental of other people. He knew it was one of Lewis's shortcomings and Anna's as well but most of the time time he let it go. "Anna was getting to me man, I follow her all over, wherever she wants to go, store after store, in one city after another. I want to go somewhere we could relax a little more."

"So why doesn't she want to go?"

"I don't know too hot, too sandy. Whatever, bottom line, I'm going with or without her."

"So what else about this other chick, is she at least hot?"

"Yeah man, black hair, intense green eyes." He knew that was all Lewis needed to hear. He wouldn't be interested in her intelligent eyes, soft glow of her skin and the intriguing way she handled the whole situation.

"Sure, I get it, a little tropical fling."

Jason had not really thought about that. He had not really thought of what it would mean to share a room with a woman that was not Anna. A beautiful woman at that. It certainly was not his intention to cheat on Anna. He suddenly was not sure what he was getting himself into. Could he resist, was it possible to do a nice thing for someone on a just friends term?

"No man, that was not my intention. She's sweet, said she had never been anywhere before."

"So what now you are a charity tour guide?"

"No," Jason grumbled back. He thought back to last night. Remembering her intense eyes, when their eyes locked and he felt a bolt of electricity lift his spirits. She defended him, stood up for him and she did not even know him.

"Listen man it does not matter to me what you do. Anna knows the score anyway, we all mess around a little. At least get it out of your system this way you can get married and be all sweet and faithful forever." Lewis ended that almost in hysterics.

"You're a piece of shit you know that right?" It was just a little dig that they used all the time. It was Jason's way to let Lewis know he was getting out of line but he was far from mad at his friend.

"Yeah man I know," grinning, "we're different but you are the one that invited a stranger on vacation so I'm just putting your options out there for you."

"Right whatever I'm outta here, got some things I need to take care of."

"Later man."

Jason left the club more in a funk and in a more confused state then when he came in. He should have known better that Lewis would not be helpful. This should not be so complicated, just a straight forward trip to show a woman something new. It would be fun to watch her experience things for the first time. So why was he in such turmoil over it? He was with Anna so there should be no thoughts of a fling or anything at all. But he knew there was an attraction.

He went inside a clothing store. He attempted to pick a few things that were more suited to this trip. Everything he picked though he knew Anna would not like. He could not remember the last time he picked out his own clothes. What did he like? He did not even know. The only thing he could manage to pick out was a very bright bathing suit that Anna would hate. At first he got a lot of satisfaction out of that but then it just left him confused again. One thing he did know was that he promised someone a vacation and he did not break his promises.

Chapter 2

By the time Molly left for work the next morning she was pretty well convinced that she would never see Jason again. After Katie left she had closed the computer vowing to set this daydream aside at least for the time being. She was practical and she was a realist. Everything she had achieved in her life she had done on her own with minimal help and would continue to do so.

She left her apartment and walked the few blocks to the supermarket. Just like every shift she had ever started she headed to the office to clock in and collect her cash drawer. Sophia, one of the other cashiers was already there. She gave Molly a snickering look and told her the manager wanted to see her right away. Molly knew Sophia did not like her very much. She thought Molly to be too straight laced and boring, never getting into any type of trouble. Sophia was right, Molly thought, but she had plans and Sophia would work here forever. She could not think of what her manager possibly wanted. She was sure Sophia was hoping she was getting disciplined for something. But she could not think of anything she could have done. She had worked here for ten years, was never late and was always accurate on her register within a few cents. As a matter of fact Alan, the manager had been a savior for her bending the rules and letting her work before she was old enough. She actually felt a little guilty that she would be leaving at the end of the fall semester. But true to her style she had already given Alan her notice. She calculated how much money she needed and figured out when her last day would be. Ok, so she was practical and boring but she was almost to her goal.

She shrugged her shoulders and wound her way to Alan's office. She heard two men talking and laughing in there, that definitely peaked her curiosity. She rapped lightly on the door not sure if she was interrupting something important. She was about to turn away when the door opened. Molly froze and her jaw dropped. There he was standing in her manager's office. Jason came back just like he said. She was not sure if she wanted to run away and hide or jump for joy. So she just stood there quietly, motionless.

Alan spoke first grinning at Molly. "Hey Molly, my new friend Jason and I were just talking about you needing a vacation."

Molly gave her usual response, "Allan you know I can't afford to take time off, plus I need to finish out at the daycare, I promised I would stay until the end of the summer session which is just three more weeks."

Jason jumped in and said, "already taken care of."

"What do you mean?" Molly asked in a slightly defensive tone. She was not sure how Jason knew or whether or not she liked that he was meddling in her life so much.

Allan turned to Jason and asked if he would give them a few minutes of privacy. He stepped out and when the door closed again Alan softened his tone. "I'm sorry honey, I helped him make the arrangements to clear your schedule. As far back as I can remember you have never taken a vacation. You deserve this."

"You know I just met him and I don't know anything about him."

"He seems like a good guy to me and you know I would be protective of you just as any father would be of his own daughter. I would tell you if he seemed sketchy."

Molly sat down, a little shaken, she was totally taken off guard by Jason being here. "I know I should do this Allen, in my heart. I just don't know," she added quietly.

Allan knelt down in front of her. "Go, take the opportunity, have a good time. Don't worry about money if that is what is stopping you."

"No, I'm sure I can manage it." A quick calculation in her head pushed her last day back a few weeks but it would be a worthwhile trade off. Then another image popped in her head, one of a tall blonde. "You know he has a girlfriend."

"That is his problem, not yours. You are going for you. You make the trip what you want it to be. To seek adventure, relaxation, learn a new culture, it is for you to decide. He is just giving you the means to do that."

And with those wise words Molly decided. She got up hugged Alan and said, "you are right, thank you."

As Alan walked out and Jason came back in she let some excitement build in her again. She also let herself really look at him again. He seemed more relaxed and sure of himself without Anna hanging over him.

"So are you on board?" he asked her.

Molly bit her lip and nodded. She hoped she could learn to relax around him.

"Great I'm excited. Don't worry about anything I will take care of everything. The trip is in two weeks is that okay?"

"Yeah that's great, there is just one thing though."

"No problem anything you need."

"Well I promised a friend of mine that I would see," she did not know why she was so nervous. She could not get the words out, she had never asked anyone out before not that this was a real date but it was still hard. She took a deep breath and looked up at him, "if we could spend a little time together before we left. You know make sure you don't have any really annoying habits that would drive me crazy."

He appreciated the bit of humor from her. "That's a good friend. Obviously she wants to make sure I'm trustworthy. So yes of course. Why don't we meet up for lunch later today."

"Oh, well, I'm here now because I actually have to work today." She raised her eyebrows at him. "Unless you have somehow gotten me out of work today too."

"As a matter of fact I have." He replied with a grin, arms crossed. "It was a just in case scenario we talked about."

Why not she thought, work or lunch with a good looking guy. That was a fairly easy decision. "Ok then but I need some time to change."

"Of course." He grabbed a piece of paper and wrote down an address. "Meet me here at one this afternoon. Is that enough time?"

"Sure, see you then."

As soon as Jason left she sat back down swallowing everything that happened. It was good she did not have to work, even without the lunch date there was no way she would have been able to concentrate. Lunch date, she just realized she had nothing to wear.

Molly started ringing Katie's phone as soon as she ran out of the store. She knew she would have to ring it several times in order for her to pick up. She normally slept in Sunday mornings after her late shift at the hospital.

Finally after several attempts Katie picked up. She was not happy. "This better be good," she grumbled.

Molly answered somewhat out of breath as she was hurrying to get back to her place. "Katie, he came back. He actually showed up at work this morning."

"Who are talking about?" Katie asked in her still groggy state.

"Jason, the guy, the trip remember?" She was breathing hard, walking fast but she needed Katie to wake up and help her. She stopped and took a deep breath. "He wants to meet me for lunch, today." Her voice was raising into minor panic mode.

This woke Katie up. "You are right, this is an emergency. Ok no problem we can handle this. Where are you now?"

"About two blocks from home."

"Ok go take a long hot shower and I will be there by the time you are finished."

Molly lingered in the shower letting the hot water soothe her. It been a long time since she went on a date. That was a disastrous blind date. So it was not the guys fault he was allergic to just about everything but she did not have to hear about every last detail. She finally drew the line when he started talking about his digestive system on a way too personal level.

So at least this was not a real date. Just a get to know you lunch get together. A lunch get together with a really hot guy. Sounds like a date. She decided to keep it light, not too personal, just enough information to go by to make the trip comfortable with him.

As Molly was wrapping her hair in a towel Katie was buzzing her bell. Katie clearly had not put any thought into her own appearance. Her long curls were thrown up into a crazy ponytail and she had on gym shorts and a well worn t shirt. And no make up, that was a rare sight. She dragged a very stuffed duffle bag behind her.

"Yikes Katie you're looking a little rough this morning."

"This is about you, not me. So what time are you meeting?"

"One, downtown."

"Shit, not a lot of time but we can do this."

Molly did not think she was that much of a wreck. She watched Katie throw all sorts of things out of her bag, makeup nail polish, clothes, lotions. She wondered where the clothes came from. Katie was a bit bigger than Molly. Part of it was the bigger bust, the other part was the fact the that Katie's mother still cooked amazing home cooked meals every night. "Where did you get all these clothes?"

"I rummaged though my brothers closets."

"What? Are they secret cross dressers that I don't know about?" Molly commented smiling. Her brothers were probably the most manly macho crew she knew.

"Don't let them here you say that. You know they've had lots of girlfriends over. I figured some of them must have left something behind." Katie picked up Molly's hand and shook her head at her rough looking unpolished nails. "We'll start with your nails then get you dressed then do your hair and makeup."

Katie started the mani pedi and Molly let herself relax. It was nice to have someone take care of her. She knew she neglected her nails and most everything else about herself. She needed to be neat and presentable. Her nails were clipped short out of practicality. She was either tapping on the cash register or helping little kids with craft projects. For her, nail polish was a waste of time, it started chipping off the day after she applied it. Her toenails were equally neglected as they were always covered with comfortable shoes. She lived on her feet except at school. Between walking everywhere and her two jobs she could not wear sandals. She owned one pair, probably outdated, maybe she would buy a new pair so she could paint her nails.

"So where are you meeting?" Katie asked as she carefully applied polish to her toenails.

"I'm not sure. He just gave me a midtown address."

"Hmm makes it hard to pick out an outfit." Molly could tell her brain was running a mile a minute. That was fine with her. For once in her life she was going to let someone else take care of her. Well to an extent anyway, Katie could get a little more daring with the clothes than Molly cared for.

"I think causal, nothing crazy, it is an afternoon meeting."

"You mean date." Katie corrected her with a wink.

"No, casual get to know you get together," Molly insisted.

"Yup it's a date," Katie smiled at her after checking her work.

Molly let it go.

"Ok sit and let your nails dry and I will look through your clothes." She started in the small closet. After pushing all the clothes aside she asked, "hey where is that black halter top you bought the last time we went shopping?"

Molly coughed a little and said sheepishly, "I returned it."

Katie have her a little glare and moved to the dresser.

"Sorry, I needed the money more than I needed the top." Her clothes, just like her nails, were practical. Jeans, polos and sweaters were perfect for the daycare, the supermarket and school. She had little need for anything else. Katie would drag her out sometimes to go shopping but it was mostly to give her opinion on what Katie was buying for herself. Occasionally she would be talked into buying something for herself. And she did sometimes return them.

"I told you, you never know when you need some nice going out clothes."

"I know but I haven't needed them, until now that is."

Katie kept rummaging and pulled out of few bottoms and tops. Then she went and dumped the clothes in the duffle on the floor. She grabbed a skirt and top and tossed them at Molly. "Here try these on and be careful of your nails."

Katie kept at her search while Molly changed. She walked over to her bed with the clothes a little skeptical. There did not seem to enough material in her hand to cover her left shoulder let alone anything else. She got changed in the corner. Being a studio there was no place to go for privacy except the bathroom. Molly did not care though, Molly and Katie quit being shy around each other back in middle school when they first met. She was trying to get the skirt to go lower when she said, "I don't think so, way too short."

"Yeah you are right. Looks too eager." She was still laying clothes together on the floor, kind of like dressing paper dolls.

"Not a date." Molly reminded her as she peeled the tight skirt off her.

"Umm hmm," she handed Molly another outfit.

A minute later, "this one just hangs on me." It was a sundress that was clearly made for someone with a much larger chest.

A few more changes and Molly was smiling at herself. It was simple, casual and fit her really well. "This one is it."

"I thought you would like that. You look great, let's get started on your hair and makeup."

Molly sat down in front of her and let the transformation continue. Katie blew out her hair and added a little curl to the ends. She did very basic makeup with mascara, eyeliner and lip gloss. When Molly saw herself in the mirror she almost broke down in tears. She held it back though since she did not want to add black streaks to her new look. Katie knew her so well. Her eyes sparked in their simplicity. She was ready to go. She gave her best friend a huge hug and said, "thank you, I love you."

"You look gorgeous, go make him drool."

Chapter 3

Molly entered the subway station that she used on almost a daily basis. You had to go down a flight of steps outside before going in to take an elevator deep below ground. The terrain at the north end of the city was quite varied. Big freight elevators took the masses below to the platform. Sometimes there was an attendant in the elevator. If he was there she would give him a polite nod but not much else. She could not imagine sitting there all day going up and down in the grimy dimly lit box. Some of the stations were being overhauled with new tiles and artwork but it only did so much to distract from the grime and giant rats running the tracks. Still, there were worse stations and this one only had one train with one uptown and one downtown track so it was never overly crowded.

Just as she thought, there were not too many people on the subway platform, typical for a Sunday. Molly left a little early since fewer trains were running.

Also there was not an express train today so there were going to be more stops. She easily found a seat when the train arrived, it would get more crowded as they went further downtown. There were no entertainers on the train today. Sometimes she would catch break dancers, brass bands, guys selling dvds, anyone trying to make a buck. Instead she closed her eyes and let the images of palm trees, blue ocean and lush mountains drift through her mind. She had not yet asked where they were staying. Maybe she would not, that would be a nice surprise. In any case she hoped it was on the ocean.

Like an internal alarm clock, she knew when her stop was coming and she opened her eyes back to reality. The address she was given was only a few blocks from the station. She was glad to see it was still warm and sunny. A lot of people did not like summer in the city, always complaining of the heat. But for her and her sister growing up, summer meant freedom and her best childhood memories were of those summer days.

She walked the few blocks thinking of her sister but was a little confused when she reached her destination. Jason had mentioned a lunch date so she was expecting a restaurant but it seemed that this was an upscale deli. She rechecked the address and went inside to see if Jason was amongst the crowd of people.

Jason made sure to get to the deli early since he knew it was going to throw Molly off a bit. He wanted to do something different for this get to know you date, meeting, whatever it was. He wanted to keep everything open and honest with Anna and when he told her about his plan she just laughed and said whatever. If you want to drip in sweat the whole day go for it. It made him hesitate for a minute thinking maybe they should just sit in an air conditioned restaurant. He decided to stick to his plan. It was more intimate and something he had been wanting to do but Anna did not.

Jason grabbed a few of the menus and picked out what he was going to order. He came here occasionally so it did not take him long to decide. As it started to get more crowded he kept a closer eye on the door. He checked it every time it opened. He decided to go outside to see if he could catch her coming down the street but just as he reached the door he felt a tap on his shoulder. He turned around and took a double take. Molly was standing there looking even more beautiful than he could have imagined. Her eyes were sparkling, her long jet black hair softly framed her face. Her skinny black capris and shimmering pink cami were understated yet the perfect outfit. He appreciated her slim yet athletic body. She took his breath away. He had to get himself under control, the date, meeting, was just starting.

"Oh hi Molly," he managed to get out, "I guess I did not see you."

"Well you know, my cashiers uniform was in the laundry so this was the only thing I had left." They both laughed at that.

Molly was relieved. The joke calmed some of the tension she was feeling between them. She had to keep her emotions under control since Anna was in the picture. Focus on the trip she kept telling herself. Of course that was hard when Jason was so good looking. He was still wearing long pants though, but a more casual outfit. She was starting to wonder if he had awful legs. She looked back up to his eyes and managed a smile. "This is not quite what I was expecting."

"Well I thought we would take advantage of this beautiful day so we are going on a picnic." He smiled at her as he handed her a menu. "Pick whatever you want."

"That sounds great." She liked the plan so far. She scanned the menu. She had not heard or tried most of what was on it so she decided to play it safe. She wanted to enjoy the day including the food. She picked a basic club sandwich with fixings, a side salad and a bottle of Dasani. After they picked up their order they headed outside. They were pretty close to Central Park and she figured they would walk over but instead Jason grabbed a cab. Molly rarely used cabs as it was an expense she could not afford. Since it was Jason's plans she got in and went along for the ride.

They kept the conversation light as the cab headed downtown. They talked about the record breaking high temps, the possibility of a hurricane heading towards the city. Jason mentioned something about the Yankees and Mets but Molly did not pay much attention to baseball. They zigzagged though the streets and Jason paid the fare when they reached their destination. When Molly got out she saw they were at the entrance to an elevated train track. She got very excited when she realized where they were.

"This is the High Line, right?" The High Line was an elevated train track that had recently been converted into a a park. They built walkways, seating and added landscaping. "This is great, I have been wanting to come check this out, have you been down here yet?"

He nodded as they climbed the stairs to reach the platform. "I have walked parts of it but it is not much fun by yourself."

"You have not taken Anna here?" she secretly hoped not. That was probably a little selfish but she liked the idea of sharing something with Jason that no one else had.

"No, if you had not guessed she is not much into the hot weather. She was not interested in being out here all day drenched in sweat. She promised to come out in the cooler weather."

Molly shrugged off the comment. She was glad to be here with him. And she was also glad to know that he was being honest with Anna about what they were up to. It made her feel more comfortable having everything out in the open.

She took in everything as they walked. She studied the way they built the walkway, how they strategically added benches to take advantage of certain views and alternatively added plants and trees to block certain areas. After walking for a few minutes they came to an area where there was stadium seating so they could look down on the street, this was perfect Molly thought since people watching was one of her favorite past times.

They found some space and sat in comfortable silence while they ate their food. She was glad they had incorporated shade into this space. She turned to Jason, "speaking of sweating, do you ever wear shorts?"

It seemed odd to her that Jason had to think about that for a few minutes. "I have a few pairs so yes, on occasion." He was getting defensive.

"It was just a question, not a criticism." Molly finished her salad and started on her sandwich. It was stuffed with meats and lettuce and tomatoes. She had to squish it down to be able to bite into it. She hoped she did not make a complete mess of herself.

She looked over at Jason, he was just nibbling at his sandwich staring out into the distance, she wondered what he was thinking. She did not mean to hurt his feelings with the clothes, she was just curious really. He did finally respond though.

"Well with work I guess I don't get much of a chance," he said then took a large bite of his sandwich.

That was a pretty lame answer she thought but let it go. It did not matter much to her either way. They continued to eat in silence. It was not a real comfortable silence. She needed to figure out how to get the conversation going again. They sure could not spend a whole week together, let alone an airline trip, in this kind of silence. She finished her lunch and got up to throw out her wrappers. When she sat back down she focused her attention on the people down below. There was a couple walking at a good clip. They were wearing matching workout clothes and carried gym bags. She asked, "hey Jason what do you think that couple is talking about?"

He had not been paying attention. His thoughts were all over the place. He did wonder why he had not worn something cooler on this hot day. Then he could not quite remember what shorts he did have. He watched as Molly threw out her trash. She looked great in shorts. He wondered what she would look like in a bikini. He wondered why he was having these thought and then remembered she asked him a question. He turned and focused on finding the couple in question. He was not quite sure what kind of answer she was looking for. "Hmm I don't now."

"I think she is saying she can curl more than he can." She smiled and did a pretend arm curl.

He understood now noting that her arms were also sexy and well defined with muscles. "Maybe, but he thinks he definitely looks better while lifting the weight."

"She definitely thinks her butt is way better than his."

Jason gave her a quick sultry look thinking Molly had the best butt of anyone. He laughed and was getting into this game. "Ok what about two guys walking the dogs."

Oh this was a good one Molly thought. One was a poodle and one was a yorkie. The yorkie was dressed in a princess costume and the poodle looked like bat-dog. "Well Foo foo's owner does not believe they should be going to Sparkle's party. Sparkles has been causing trouble at the dog park. She keeps sniffing bat-dog and everyone know Foo foo belongs to bat-dog."

"Yes but we already bought the costumes and sent the dogs to the spa. Besides you know Sparkle's dad just got over a rough relationship so we need to be there."

"Fine but don't be all dramatic when Foo foo shows Sparkles who is the top bitch." Molly flicked her finger and crossed her arm playing into the character.

Jason was laughing again and once again could not take his eyes off Molly. He enjoyed her storytelling. He was impressed how she easily rattled off scenarios. She was funny but so matter of fact getting into character, rolling her eyes and snapping her fingers. He looked down at the street and found a typical tourist couple looking at the maps. "What do you think of them? I say they are staying at the Best Western, they have seen lady liberty, took in the show Chicago and bought ten pounds worth of taxi colored m and ms."

Molly studied the couple for a moment. She figured they had another side to them that no one would know about. "Yeah now they are figuring out how to get to 42 street to buy some kinky leather outfits and fuzzy handcuffs to take to their next swingers party."

Jason's jaw dropped but quickly joined Molly in hysterics. They carried on with the scenarios for quite some time. Seeing who could come up with the most outrageous stories.

Molly was starting to feel at ease with Jason. He was relaxed and enjoying her game but as much as she was having a good time she also felt it was time to head home. She stood up and stretched. "Thank you Jason I had a great time today. I know this whole thing has been crazy but I feel a lot better about this trip. I trust you and feel comfortable going with you."

"Good I'm glad I passed your no weirdness requirements."

"Well unless you have some weird thing with your legs that you won't wear shorts I guess we are going on a trip."

"Ha ha, no problems with the legs. This trip is going to be great and there will be no backing out." For either one of them he added silently.

They headed down to street level and when Jason started motioning for a cab Molly stopped him. "I think there is a subway station a few blocks from here."

"We can take a cab, I don't mind." He stepped off the curb to flag one down.

"Jason I live over a hundred blocks from here plus then you have to come back to wherever you live." She could not understand his hesitation. "How about you walk me to the nearest station then we can both make our way home from there."

He agreed but somewhat reluctantly. That meant their day would end quicker. He really wanted to see her again. They had fun but he did not truly learn anything about her other than her great sense of humor. When they reached the subway entrance they turned to each other but neither seemed to know want to say.

"Thanks again Jason. If you would just call me with flight times." She reached into her purse to grab her metro card since she did not know what else to do or say at this point.

He wanted to delay but he knew it was Sunday and they both had to work the next day. He hesitated, stalling, absorbing her image into his memory. Then he heard himself saying, "actually I was thinking we could go out again. Dinner this time maybe. I still don't know much about you."

Molly was still debating on how much personal information they should exchange based on his current relationship status but she really wanted to see him again and was glad he asked first. "Ok, but it will have to wait until next Sunday night if that is ok."

They made plans for him to pick her up at her place, they gave each other a quick hug and went on their separate ways.

Chapter 4

The following weekend Molly and Katie skipped their Saturday morning meeting and opted to go shopping on Sunday instead. They met early and had breakfast at the local diner. They met up early enough so they would not have to wait for a table. Katie also had a full day of shopping planned. After trying to find just one outfit for her last date she knew they had to start from scratch for this trip. Katie was anxious to hear about that date. They kept playing phone tag and Molly would not tell her much over voice mail.

"I can't believe how busy work has been this week, tell me everything about your date."

Molly had given up on not calling it a date. She had not said much to her best friend about it. She wanted to tell her in person. "We had a picnic at the High Line Park."

"That's different," she managed between forkfuls of eggs.

"Yeah it was a lot of fun." She went on to tell her about the food and story telling.

"So no weird habits?"

Molly was not sure if she should mention the pants thing but then she did not want to keep anything from her. It probably did not mean much anyway. "No except it was pretty hot last weekend and he seems to have an issue with his clothes." Molly waited for a response as she spread jelly on her toast. Katie just raised her eyebrows waiting for a further explanation. "I'm sure it's nothing. He was complaining about being hot the night we met and then he was wearing long pants again. He said he had no issues with his legs," she added in his defense.

Katie contemplated this for a moment. "His girlfriend probably dressed him. He looked good right?"

Molly nodded, "he mentioned that she does that for him sometimes."

"I am sure it is nothing, so now you are going to dinner tonight?"

Molly nodded without looking up.

Katie watched her. She knew her friend well, she was hiding something. She looked at her friend square in the eyes as she said, "you like him."

Molly wondered if it was that obvious. It must be since she had not been on a date in years. The problem was that she shouldn't like him. Not as more than a friend anyway. Besides his obvious good looks, it was really too early too tell. "I don't know, I don't know him very well."

"But you like him," Katie said pushing her.

"Let's see, good looking, fun, good date choice, oh did I mention he has a girlfriend."

"She sounds like a bitch to me, I say go for it."

"What do you mean go for it?" Molly knew what she meant. It was much easier for Katie. She was much more outgoing and experienced with the whole dating scene. Besides the fact that Molly had no intentions of breaking up a relationship.

"Jason of course, go to the island and have some fun, what do you have to lose?"

"I don't know, he's involved, I'm not sure I am capable of that."

"Well you know what they say what happens in Vegas stays in Vegas, it does not have to be any different on the island. It's a week, indulge."

Molly chopped her pancakes to little bits and smiled at Katie, "well if he comes on to me I'm not sure I will be able to resist." That was definitely true. She could not stop thinking about his eyes and his smile. Just as he did not know her, she did not know him that well. Maybe she would not like his personality all that much and then it would be easy. She did not really believe that though.

"Darling when we are done shopping he won't be able to resist you." Katie finished her breakfast and motioned for the check. She was ready to hit the stores.

"Thats what I'm afraid of." Molly on the other hand was a little hesitant about shopping. Besides spending the money she barely had, their styles were very different.

"Well if nothing happens with Jason at least find some island boy to have fun with."

Molly laughed, "why are you so adamant I have a fling? Maybe I just want to go enjoy the nature and beautiful sights."

"Exactly, beautiful sights, handsome men with washboard abs." Katie turned to Molly after she paid the bill, "I know palm tree, sunsets, waterfalls, whatever, all boring without a little man eye candy to go with it. Go have fun, you earned it."

Molly knew her friend was right. She just needed to figure out what her own definition of fun was going to be.

The fall fashions were already out which meant bargains on summer clothes. Molly was determined to stick to a budget. She reluctantly pulled money out of her savings account vowing to pay it back after the trip with a few extra shifts at the market.

They hit all of Katie's favorite shops. Molly tried on everything, dresses, shorts, tops, shoes, bathing suits. Katie had her in and out of so many dressing rooms Molly was starting to get dizzy. They went back and forth trying to compromise on styles. Katie thought short and low cut. Molly wanted a little more coverage. They were eventually able to make some compromises.

Picking out the day wear was easy enough but the bathing suits were a little harder. "I don't understand what is wrong with the one piece I picked," she yelled out to Katie.

"Old lady frumpy."

"What if I want to go for a run on the beach."

"You, run? Not likely."

Molly knew Katie was right. She sorted through the pile of suits and tossed out the ruffles, polka dots, thongs. "Hey Katie no dental floss please."

She settled on a black string bikini that had a some beadwork attached. It matched her hair and contrasted her fair skin without washing her out. She put in on and looked at herself in the mirror. She had to admit to herself that she looked good in it. She smiled as she walked out of the dressing room to show Katie.

"Now that is what I'm talking about girlfriend, you look sexy in that." She smiled and handed her more to choose from.

With renewed energy she went back to the dressing room and picked out another bathing suit in a deep red color that added a nice contrast to her black hair. Katie gave approval on the second suit. Molly paid for her suits and they headed out again.

Katie wanted to go to another store to pick out some evening dresses. Molly was not sure how dressy she should go. She figured there would be some opportunities to go out at night but was not sure if it would be. by herself or with someone. She figured it would be better to be prepared.

By the time they hit the last store Molly was getting tired. They managed to agree on a few dresses of varying lengths including one dress she absolutely loved which she bought despite its high price tag. She thought she was done when Katie threw one last pile into the dressing room. "Make sure you try on the black one."

This must have been some kind of plot since she hated the rest of the pile. She liked the black dress but it did not seem to fit with the tropical vacation theme. She sighed and tried it on anyway. It was a simple black cocktail dress with spaghetti straps and simple floral pattern embossed onto it. She did like it but, "Katie this is not exactly tropical vacation dress," she commented as she walked out of the dressing room.

"No but it is perfect for going out to dinner tonight."

With all the shopping she had forgotten about her plans for tonight. "I don't think I could eat in this, there is no room to spare." She sucked in her stomach to prove she was right.

"Stop that, you have the flattest stomach. This dress is meant to show off your fabulous body."

"Don't you think it's too much though?" She did not want to be too obvious to Jason.

"No."

Well it was dinner after all, she could dress up a little if she wanted to. She looked at the price tag and sighed. It would put her over her budget.

Katie caught her sigh, "don't worry about the price, I am buying this one for you."

"Katie you don't have to do that."

"I want to, please let me. Besides every woman needs a little black cocktail dress in her closet."

Molly was still hesitant. "Are you sure it's not too much though? It's just supposed to be another get to know you more dinner."

"Yup he will get to know more of you in that dress."

"Ha ha," Molly gave her friend a light punch in the shoulder, "won't it give the wrong impression?"

"I don't know, what impression do you want to give him?"

"I don't know." she did like the dress though and since Katie offered to pay for it, "ok you can buy it but I will think about wearing it tonight."

"Ok, at least take it with you and no returning it, or anything you bought today."

"I promise I won't, thank you Katie."

Downtown Jason stifled a yawn as he waited outside the dressing room where Anna was trying on clothes. She never came out to show him what she was trying on. It would probably be more interesting for him if she did. But he knew it would be dangerous territory if he offered an opinion anyway. She claimed she liked to surprise him but he knew the truth that his opinion was not that important to her. He was the business man and she was the fashion expert anyway. That is why she always picked out his clothes. She was always showcasing the latest styles for both men and women. They never were matched exactly but they always complimented each other. In other words he could never look better than her. Not that he did, she was beautiful and he did like that she cared about how she looked. Sometimes it was frustrating and time consuming but he knew if she looked good he would also.

As they left with another bag to go to another store he asked, "so tell me why you need more new clothes." He was still irritated that she turned down this trip with him. He was also irritated that he could not get Molly out of his head. It was an unwanted and unneeded attraction that was complicating his life right now. He hoped he would get over it tonight, he was sure it was just a passing feeling and then he could get back to normal.

Anna sighed and said again, "I told you I have nothing to wear in Italy."

Jason thought of the huge closets she kept at his place and at hers that were full of clothes but he knew better than to argue. "I thought you were going to go shopping in Milan darling."

"Yes but I need to look my best over there."

"You always look great honey."

She gave him a sweet smile, the kind of smile you would give to a child that knew nothing of what the adult was speaking, "you know I have to stay on top of the fashion industry and I won't be seen in last years clothes especially in one of the fashion capitals of the world."

"I thought we lived in the fashion capital."

"Honey you just stick to your job and let me handle the clothes. I know, when we get back from Italy we can have a party to show off my new clothes and to celebrate us, okay?" She gave him a wink and a smile.

Jason knew what she meant in a way. They had been together for six years. They met in college and agreed to spend a few years establishing their careers. They kept separate apartments but rarely spent the night alone. He knew it was time to move on in their relationship, she was obviously ready. He looked at her, they were a good match. He relaxed and felt better about things. Although he had not planned on the time or money for Italy he would make it work to make Anna happy. He did want to make her happy.

"You know I have not actually agreed to go to Italy with you. And you still can go to St. Lucia with me." He said giving her a little sad puppy smile.

"What about your little friend."

"If you change your mind I will figure something else out for her."

"You would do that?" she asked with an eyebrow up.

"For you, yes." Jason felt a little twinge of nervousness waiting for her to answer. If Anna agreed to go he would let Molly out of his thoughts and after the trip, out of his life.

"That's sweet but no thanks," she snipped at him before entering another store.

Jason had a lot of mixed feelings. Disappointment and anger with Anna and the excitement of going with Molly. He just smiled and gave Anna a soft kiss following her through another set of gold trimmed doors.

"Come on darling now we need to find you some new clothes."

Jason sighed and followed her to the men's department. There was not much left to say and there was no getting out of going to the men's department. At least he had dinner to look forward to.

Chapter 5

As was his usual custom Jason took a cab from his midtown apartment to Molly's uptown address. He did not remember being so far north when he and Anna went to the dinner party. Molly mentioned it would be a costly cab ride but he was okay with it, it was faster anyway. He imagined she did not use cabs too often. He knew it was a bit of a luxury, short of having your own personal car and driver, and he knew plenty of people that did. Some day Anna might push him in that direction. He was not sure he could justify that expense other than actually employing the driver. At least here he could be alone with his thoughts and not worry about beggars, germs and getting lost in the labyrinth of trains and stations.

His thoughts were solely about Molly. He wondered what she would wear and how it would affect him. It should not affect him at all. He should be able to handle a female relationship that was not Anna but it was getting a little difficult. Perhaps this evening would help clear his emotions.

The cab stopped at her corner and he paid the fare as he got out. It seemed he was only a few blocks from where they met just a few nights ago. He took a quick look around and noted that it was mostly a residential neighborhood. There seemed to be a nice park nearby as well. The buildings were pretty similar but they seemed clean and well kept. He was glad she lived somewhere that seemed pretty safe and friendly.

The only thing that he did not care for was that there was no doorman but he knew those buildings came with a premium. But again, the lobby was clean and well kept which meant the residents cared about their homes. He took the elevator and knocked on Molly's door right at 7 pm just as they planned. He did not expect that she would be ready but he at least could be on time. Either way was fine, Molly was worth waiting for. His plan tonight was to get to know her on a more personal level. He already liked what he knew about her. Beside her beauty, she was funny and confident but shy at the same time. She would make a great travel companion but that would have to be all.

The door opened only a minute after he knocked. Molly came out in a little shimmering body hugging black dress. As he felt a wave of heat rush through his center he added sexy to that list.

"You look great," he managed to get out after what seemed like forever.

Molly smiled but dropped her eyes as she turned to lock the door.

"Are you ready?" he asked her quizzically, "do you need more time?"

"No I'm ready," she replied dropping her keys in her purse. She noticed the confused look on his face and just lifted her eyebrows.

"Oh well I'm just used to the whole fashionably late thing."

"Well I'm not fashionable so we can go."

Could have fooled me Jason thought to himself. He let her go first not as a gentlemanly move, he wanted to get a look at the soft curves of her back end. He watched her take a few swaying steps down the hallway when she stumbled in her heels. He jumped forward to grab her by the elbow to steady her.

Molly cracked up laughing. Most woman would have been embarrassed but she did not care. "Shows you how often I wear heels," she commented to no one in particular.

Molly did notice that Jason's grip had moved from her elbow to her hand. She did not know if he was just being kind to help her balance but she did not care. Her fingers tingled with warmth and she liked the feeling. It also made her nervous knowing they could be heading into dangerous emotional and physical territory. She kept hearing Katie's voice in her mind, have fun, return to your life later. She did know one thing that her life would likely be forever changed after this trip. At this point any change would probably do her good. She would still be a little cautious with Jason but would go with whatever happened.

Molly had managed to get out of the building without any further stumbles. Jason noticed he was still holding her hand. He liked the way it felt but he knew he should ignore the tingles he felt in his fingers, the serenity it gave his whole being. He dropped her hand reluctantly and shoved both in his pockets. Why would she get so dressed up for this anyway? They were just supposed to get to know each other a little more. This was definitely a physical show and he kept thinking about dessert. He gritted his teeth to try to stop his thoughts of her undressed.

"It's a beautiful night, you don't mind walking do you?" Molly could see she interrupted Jason's thoughts. He was looking at her but she could not tell what he was thinking.

"Sure, just lead the way," he commented with little emotion. Molly thought his mood had taken an abrupt downturn, especially after pulling his hand out of hers. She was not sure what she did wrong, hopefully he would snap out of it soon otherwise she would be making some sort of excuse to end the night early.

They walked the few blocks in silence. Jason tried to relax and calm his nerves. He wanted to enjoy the evening. He did open the door for her showing that he still had manners despite his mood. The restaurant was small and dimly lit. It had small intimate tables. The walls were covered with drapery and there were pillows everywhere. Despite his best efforts he was having trouble relaxing. Not only could he not stop staring at Molly but now he would be seated very close to her with a high likelihood their bodies would brush against each other.

As Molly checked in he stood with his arms folded, lips pursed tightly together. Molly looked at him, head tilted, "are you okay?"

"Fine" was his only comment

Molly had called ahead for a reservation so they were seated quickly despite the increasing number of patrons at the front. They were seated at a small table along the wall. Jason motioned for her to sit in the comfy bench side while he took the chair. She did notice that he had nice manners despite his irritation. She did not get it, she thought this would be a nice place to talk where they would not have to yell over a loud crowd of people.

They both studied the menu and still sat in silence when Jason suddenly put his menu down and looked at her with cool eyes. "Do you always dress up like this for a casual dinner?"

Molly was taken aback but she gave him the same cool glare back. "Katie picked this out for me. Besides

I don't go out often, it is nice to dress up once in a while." Molly was a little hurt at his reaction to her dress. Well so be it she thought, she felt good and was determined to at least enjoy a nice meal.

They placed their orders including glasses of wine. They both sipped at the wine and started to relax somewhat.

"So is it that you don't go out much or you don't date much?" To him there was a big difference and he was curious. Not that the answer mattered, much anyway, okay maybe a little.

"Neither really, I hang out with Katie but not too many other people."

Hmm, not the answer he was expecting, he pressed her for more of an explanation. "Why not?"

She shrugged her shoulders and took another sip of the wine. "I don't know, I'm busy all the time."

She seemed to be getting just slightly uncomfortable but if he was going to get to know her he needed, wanted more information, besides what else could she possibly be doing. "All the time?" he stressed the word all.

"How about a full time job, a part time job and part time school." She replied a little more sharply than she intended. She softened a little before adding, "but I'm on break from school right now."

Jason was impressed, overwhelmed, confused yet again. "Smart, funny and beautiful, anything else I should know?"

Molly bit her lip, she was so jittery. No man had ever given her such wonderful compliments before but it came across a bit snippy so she was not sure if it was even meant to be a compliment. She could feel the tension rising between them so she decided to take it back a notch to put them more at ease. "How about boring, plan everything to the penny, did I mention I never go out?"

"Did I mention sexy?" Was that crossing a line, probably but it just slipped out, Jason thought to himself. Molly looked down but he could see a little smile unfolding.

Their meals came and they ate in silence. Jason felt a little better but still unsure of himself and even what she intended, she seemed to be flirting with him in her own quiet way. His irritation started coming back. She knew he had a girlfriend so was she purposely going after him. If she was it was totally inappropriate.

He put his fork down and glared at her again. "Do you keep getting dressed up to flirt with me? Obviously you know I'm involved so what are trying to accomplish?" he asked her straight out.

That stung and she could feel her eyes watering slightly. Maybe this was a bad idea, the whole trip, the dress. She knew she should keep her distance but she was so attracted to him. The question stung at her and she bit her tongue to fight back a tear. He was right though, she had no business interfering with his relationship. Except that Anna was a bitch, if she wasn't they would not even be here tonight. That thought gave her a bit of confidence. "I told you it feels good to dress up once in a while and I am not apologizing for the way I look." She took another bite of her food and casually added, "besides you are just as guilty of flirting when you told me I look sexy."

"It was just an obvious observation." Except that it affected his total physical being.

"And as far as Anna goes she is all wrong for you."

"And is that just an observation?" he challenged back with eyebrows raised and arms crossed.

"No," she said just as matter of fact as he had.

"So now are you going to tell me why?"

"Do you want me to?"

No, his current relationship was just fine, so why was he so attracted to another woman? "Fine tell me why!"

"Let's see, she won't take a trip of your choosing. I bet you only go where she wants."

"We went skiing together," he was quick to comment.

Ok point lost Molly thought, but she had more.

"Except she insisted on going to Aspen when I wanted to go to Whistler for the better snow."

Point gained back. "She spends too much of your money." Ok no comment. "She dresses you in clothes you hate."

"These are nice clothes."

"Whatever you say." That was all she really knew about her but it was enough. "Well it's your relationship so it's your problem to live with or not. Some men want to be led around by the hand, I want a man who can think for himself. I do not care how you choose to live your life as long as you are happy with it. In any case, I am going on this trip to have fun. That is my plan, so far I have enjoyed your company and I think we can have fun together but if not I can manage on my own."

He could not believe how critical she was of Anna or even of him. But when he thought about it she was right about everything. Now he could not believe she figured this out in just a few meetings. Did it all really bother him or was he used to it for the last six years? So was Molly just so different and that is why he saw it now? He was not sure but he did know he did not intend for Molly to wonder around St. Lucia by herself. "I don't thinks that's what you want."

Molly was ready to put an end to this course of conversation. "You want to know if I'm flirting with you. Maybe but I don't really know what I'm doing. Look Jason you are good looking, fun to be with, you laugh at my lame jokes, you have great manners. What's not to like?"

"Apparently the fact that I let everyone decide things for me," he replied a little quietly.

"No one told you to invite me on this trip."

"True."

"Why don't we just enjoy each others company then and not worry about anything else."

"Ok," he replied somewhat relieved but seeing no real answer to his feelings towards her.

They finished up their dinners and agreed to give up their table and sit at the bar. Neither one of them was ready to end the night. They had their wine glasses refilled and found some stools at the end of the bar. They were even closer together with knees touching but they both seemed more at ease. Jason decided to get back to the subject of finding more about Molly's life.

"So what are you studying?"

"I am finishing my masters in elementary education."

"Wow, what grade do you want to teach?"

"I think fourth or fifth grade. It's a good age to really make an impression, set kids on a good track."

"So you want to teach more underprivileged kids?"

"Yeah, I know I can't save them all, but even if I reach a few then it will be worth it."

"You said you were off from school right now but you graduate after the fall semester."

"It is typically a five year program but it's taken me seven and a half including summers, except this one."

"Why so long?" he was definitely curious, intrigued and impressed.

"I was lucky and got scholarships to cover most of my tuition but I still had to support myself. I started out taken more classes but then I had a great opportunity to take over payments on my apartment so I took it. It slowed me down in classes since I had to work more but it was worth it. So now I am almost done."

"Then what, when will you start teaching?"

"I actually will be a full time substitute at the school this school year and then next year I will hopefully get my own class."

"What about your jobs now?"

"Since it is the end of summer my last day at the daycare will be right before leave. The supermarket, probably sometime after Christmas. I gave my notice to Allan for a time frame but as it gets closer I will figure out exactly how long I need to keep working there. I can't wait to graduate, Jason, I have been focused for so long."

"It's an amazing accomplishment."

"Thanks," she flashed him a genuine smile.

"Your family must be very proud as well." She had not mentioned any so he figured that would be a good way to learn about others in her life. But it was not quite the response he expected. She turned a little sullen and looked away.

"I have not spoken to my family in years."

"I'm sorry," she shrugged but offered no explanation, "any siblings?" he pressed a little more.

"Julie, my sister, but she is not here anymore." She took a long sip of her wine not willing to share anymore so she turned the subject on him. "So what about your career?"

He was disappointed that she would not talk anymore but he would not press. "I'm an investment broker."

"Hmm it's been a rough economy but you seem to be doing pretty well."

"My dad has been really helpful. He was often criticized for not being overly aggressive but he helped me make some good choices that have paid off."

"So your dad is in the same business?"

"Yeah he taught me early on. He was always reading The Wall Street Journal and one day I asked what he was reading and ever since then he taught me to watch the market, stay up on current affairs and world events and politics. He explained the value of long and short term investments."

"Makes sense. So then that is want you always wanted to do?"

"I guess. I'm the only boy in my family so I just followed in my dads footsteps."

He seemed a little uneasy but she did not mean it as a criticism. "I did not say it was a bad thing. Most dads love it if their kids went into the same business. I just meant did you have any dreams of being a pro athlete or a rock star, anything like that."

He thought about that for a minute. "Not that I recall. How about you?"

"No I was a realist early on. So you like your job then?"

"I do. It's a challenge and because of my dad I was able to keep quite a few people from losing too much money."

She raised her glass, "well then that is an accomplishment to be proud of as well."

He met her glass and they toasted to their successes.

Jason was feeling good. He was so focused on their conversation that he forgot about his emotional conflicts. He loved her passion, her enthusiasm for life. She set goals and accomplished them. She was fun, strong, independent and caring. He still wondered about her family and he hoped he would find out soon but this was a good start.

Molly rarely shared so much of her life and she was not ready to talk about her family especially Julie, not just yet anyway. It was a bit of a rough start to the evening but she was really enjoying herself now. She could see glimpses of a side of Jason he probably does not show often. She hope to continue to open him up some more but for tonight she was tired.

"Jason can you walk me home?"

"Absolutely, no way I would let you go by yourself."

"I can take care of myself."

"I know," and he really did, "but you don't always have to."

That sounded so simple in her ears but it was more true than she ever let herself consider. "You are right Jason, it really means a lot to me actually that you care."

Jason jumped off his stool and held out his hand to help her step down. She took his hand this time not worrying about the warm tingle that travelled up his arm and led him outside.

The night was warm but there was a light rain falling. "Do you want me to grab a cab?"

"No, I like the warm rain." She smiled at childhood memories but kept her thoughts to herself for now. She commented instead on how she loved the smell of the moist air and how alive she felt as if renewed by the rain washing bad things away.

He wondered what those bad things would be but kept quiet just enjoying Molly enjoying the rain. If he had been with Anna they would be in a cab and she would be worrying about her make up running. They reached her door way too soon but he knew she had work in the morning. He looked at her again, her hair soaked but she still looked beautiful.

Molly lingered in front of her building entrance. It turned out to be lovely evening. She was looking forward to spending more time with Jason. "I don't know how I am going to make it through this week." Her eyes got wide with excitement.

"Well you can start by packing this dress," he grinned at her.

"Yeah I might have a few other new things I can pack. Katie took me shopping today."

"Hmm I was out shopping with Anna today as well. Claimed we had nothing for Italy."

"Really? Interesting we did not run in to each other seeing that I was on Fifth Avenue myself." She burst out laughing but stopped realizing Jason did not find this humorous.

"Sorry, could not help myself, I really did need some vacation clothes though."

"Hey you are entitled. Anna just happens to have several closets full of clothes."

"Well you know women and their shopping."

"That I do. So what are the chances of a cab coming by here?" He did not want to get back into a discussion about his relationship with Anna.

"One will come eventually but the subway station is just two blocks away."

"Ok thanks."

They gave each other a quick hug and said good night. He lucked out and saw a cab just drop off it's passenger and ran over to it. Molly watched him go in wonder.

Chapter 6

Jason was rummaging through his closet trying to decide what to bring on the trip. Nothing he owned seemed appropriate. Of course he did not even know what that was. Anna usually did the packing for him but he insisted he take care of this himself. Anna was sitting in the bed reading the latest Vogue. He knew she was pretending not to pay attention but he could feel her grimacing at his choices. Finally he turned to her, "what do you care what I wear since you won't be there."

She just shrugged in response but then looked up at him, "well if I have to see you off at the airport I at least get to pick out what you wear that day." He sighed, he did not want to start an argument.

He threw a few more things in his bag in a hurry as he was supposed to meet Lewis and some others at a local bar in a short while. "Are you still coming with me tonight?"

"I think I'm coming down with a headache," she said as she buried her head back in the magazine.

"But we won't see each other for a week."

"I need my rest for Italy."

"It's just a few drinks, I want you to come, please?" He gave her his sad eyes look.

"I'm really not in the mood honey, why don't you invite your little friend, what's her name again? Melanie?"

"Molly," he said softly. It seemed like he was seeing more of Molly recently than his own girlfriend. He sat down on the bed next to Anna and brushed his hand along her cheek. "It's just that we have not seen much of each other lately."

"I know but we will have a week together when you get back and you will have all my attention." She reached forward and gave him a sultry kiss. "Go on have a good time."

"Okay see you later."

"I love you darling." Anna blew him a kiss but quickly went back to her reading.

"Love you too," he answered back despite feeling a little rejected.

Molly was also in her apartment packing. She could not believe the trip was only two more days away. She had all her new clothes laid out on the floor. She had to remove all the tags and make sure she had enough matching outfits. She read that if you rolled the clothes they were less likely to wrinkle. She had borrowed a suitcase from Katie and was carefully placing each item in a good spot so that everything laid evenly trying to maximize space. She did not want to overpack, anticipating bringing home a few souvenirs, but Katie said it was best to be prepared for every occasion and every mood. She remembered how Katie winked and smiled at her when she said that so what she really meant was to be prepared if something happened between her and Jason. She was imaging him in a bathing suit coming out of the water when her phone rang. She sighed as she let the image go and answered the phone without looking at the caller I.D.

"Hello?"

"Hey Molly it's Jason."

"Oh hi, what's up?"

"Just doing some packing, how about you?"

"Same thing actually."

"Well I was getting ready to have a few drinks with some friends and thought I would call to see if you wanted to join me."

"What about Anna? Isn't she going with you." She would not go if the bombshell beauty was going to be there.

"She's not feeling well, as a matter of fact she suggested I ask you."

That was weird she thought, not really knowing what to say.

When Molly did not respond he added, "it's just a few drinks, I know you have to work tomorrow so we don't have to stay out long."

What would Katie say Molly thought to herself. She laughed that was easy, go out have fun, and it was another chance to see him again. "Ok but only if you meet me at the exit to the subway station."

"Of course. See you soon."

She had a few things still laid out on the floor. She picked a simple flowing summer dress, put on the basic make up Katie showed her and headed out the door.

Forty five minutes later she emerged onto street level. As promised Jason was waiting for her. She tingled all over as he gazed at her with an appreciative grin.

He gave her a light hug, "another new dress?"

"Yes and if we keep meeting like this you will see my whole new wardrobe before we even leave."

"I am looking forward to seeing what else you bought," he said giving her a wink. He especially wondered what kind of swimwear she would be bringing.

She smiled back but made no comment. Molly was glad to see him but a little apprehensive about meeting his friends. She assumed they would have nothing in common which was okay, she just wanted to be able to be herself.

They entered an upscale pub with dark woods and polished brass. Jason quickly found his friends and guided her over to them. Jason introduced her to the few people at the table including Lewis.

Lewis took her hand and gently kissed it while looking at her up and down. The obvious inspection made her uncomfortable. It was not the same appreciative way Jason looks at her. It was more of a hunger, I want you then I will dispose of you look. She pulled her hand back but gave him a nod and slight smile so as not appear to be rude.

"Very elegant, not quite what I was expecting." Lewis said to Jason.

"And what exactly were you expecting?" Molly asked cynically staring at him.

He held her gaze right back but then leaned back and smiled, "I don't know, I don't know many cashiers."

Was that a dig, she wondered. She decided to try to lighten the mood or else she was going home. "Well it is your lucky day since it was my night to shower, you know up in my neck of the woods we can only shower every third day. Oh and I picked the food out of my teeth too." She turned and winked at Jason to let him know she was okay before sliding into the bench that wrapped around the corner table.

Jason slid in next to Molly. He had to physically unclench his fists. He wanted to hit Lewis, first for blatantly looking her up and down and then for being judgmental. He relaxed slightly when she cracked that joke and winked at him. He wanted to reassure her further so when he sat down he grabbed her hand under the table and gave it a squeeze but he decided he would hold on to it, let her know he was on her side.

Molly relaxed also with the comfort Jason was giving her. As they were sitting there he played with her hand, running his fingers across the back of it and massaging her palm. It sent a constant electrical pulse up her arm. It made it hard to concentrate on the conversation. She pretended to pay attention but she had no idea what they were talking about. The only thing she could tell was that it was work related. They talked about market trends and how it was affecting stock prices. She became slightly more interested when the conversation turned to politics and the upcoming elections but she did want to continue to stay out of the conversation. Politics was always a volatile topic. She had no interest in a debate. She just wanted to enjoy the massage Jason was giving her hand. Molly's calm was broken when the conversation took a different turn.

"What do you think Molly," Lewis looked at her, "do you think the government should require everyone to have health insurance?"

"I think it is unfortunate that the government has to make that decision, everyone should have access to quality healthcare but a lot of people can not afford it on their own."

"Do you have insurance?"

"I do right now but I am going to have a lapse as I switch full time jobs."

"So what do you do if you get sick?"

"I do what everyone else does, I pray to hell I don't get sick. I know it seems un-American and the government is stomping on our freedoms but it is a lot cheaper to prevent disease than to treat them." She knew this from personal experience. She bit her lip to keep tears from appearing.

"It's just adding to the enormous debt the country already has."

"True but the intent is to create more competition and bring prices down."

"Maybe," Lewis eyed her with a strange intensity that made her uncomfortable. "So what about the burden of so many being on welfare. I imagine you have been on welfare at some point in your life, what was that like?"

She was so angry at his comment. She squeezed Jason's hand so hard it hurt. She hoped he would not let go otherwise it was going across Lewis' smug cheek.

She glared at him, "what makes you assume such a thing?"

Lewis shrugged off her anger, "I can't possible see how you can survive on a cashiers pay."

"Of course you don't. You could not possible imagine a life without champagne, limos, first class everything. I have everything I need with no excess."

"Sure whatever works for you." He sat back chuckling to himself. He could not quite understand why Jason was bothering with this girl except for a quick lay on the side. But it did amuse him to get her all worked up.

Jason jumped to her defense. "She works two jobs and goes to school."

"It's okay Jason," although she was glad he defended her, "no I am not, never was and don't ever plan to be on welfare. I work hard and I am proud of it."

"So you are on my side, that welfare is sucking society dry."

Molly pursed her lips, seems there was no avoiding a debate. "I never said that. While I feel there are opportunities out there and everyone should do their best to find a job sometimes it is not possible. Some people need a boost to get them through hard times."

"But people get dependent on them and our government should not support them forever. It's not my fault or responsibility."

"No?" she asked him eyebrows arched, "it seems that the greedy and selfish wealthy played a major role in the downturn of the economy."

Lewis leaned forward and equalled her intensity. "It seems to me that too many people borrowed too much money they could not pay back."

"Agreed, but banks should not have made those loans either," she consented the point. "Banks and consumers made a lot of bad decisions but now that we are here everyone needs to play a part in fixing the mess."

"Well the government should not tell us how to fix things."

"They left you alone to run things how you saw fit and see how things turned out, how are we to trust that you will fix things?"

"And you call the government accumulating huge amounts of debt fixing things?"

"No I call that keeping food on people's tables and roofs over their heads. I know you never had to wonder how you were going to pay for you next meal but there are people out there who have lost everything."

"People get what they deserve," he said nonchalantly.

That was enough. Molly stood up, "you are an ignorant, arrogant bastard and Jason I am sorry but I can no longer sit here listening to this. It was an interesting evening," she would not lie and say glad to have met you. Lewis was one person she hoped to never meet agin. She quickly made her way to the exit. She was taking deep breaths fighting her anger.

Molly ran outside ignoring Jason's pleading to wait for him. Only when she was able to breath the warm night air did she finally calm down. She still could not turn to face him. The anger was dissipating but it was being replaced by disappointment. She knew Lewis could not help he was born to better circumstances than she was but to be so critical and judgmental was an unforgivable trait in her mind. And this was a person Jason called a friend. Was that unforgivable as well?

She got her bearings and started walking briskly to the nearest subway station. Jason picked up his pace and grabbed her shoulder to turn her towards him.

"Molly, please slow down, I'm so sorry."

"It's fine," she pulled away from him again, "I just want to go home."

"Hold on, let me grab a cab, I'll go with you."

That comment set off her anger again, she faced him arms crossed against her chest. "Don't you get it? It's always cabs for you. The amount of money you spend on cabs can pay for a whole bunch of metro cards for you and other people. It can can pay for months worth of hot meals or fill the food shelves at the local shelters."

Jason grew a little cold at her criticism. "I work hard just like everyone else. I earned my money and I can splurge."

"I know you work hard Jason. I'm not denying your trips or nice clothes and apartment. But what have you given back? You guys have no true understanding of necessity versus need and you don't need to take a cab everywhere." She was done talking to him and turned away again.

Jason watched her walk off. He felt like he was punched in the gut. He was not sure if he should let her go or follow. He could not help the way he grew up but she was right that he never did really think about the way other people lived. He was not sure about his feelings right now but he was raised to be a gentleman and there was no way he was going to let her go home alone.

He caught up with her. "Hold on, I'm still going with you."

"You'll have to ride the train," she snipped at him.

"Fine."

"Fine."

They went down the stairs into the station and stopped at the ticket vending machine. She talked him into buying a monthly unlimited card in the hopes that he would use it again. She led him silently to the waiting platform. She could have explained all the different lines to him but was not much in the mood for talking. The train came and it was fairly crowded. Molly found a spot near a pole to hang on to. Jason squeezed in next to her. She wanted to pull away but there was no place to go. She closed her eyes and leaned against him. She knew they came from different worlds and she knew she would not fit into his especially with friends like Lewis. She really hoped Jason did not share his same values but he did not say much. He did defend her but did not disagree with what Lewis said. Also she did not give him much of a chance either. She really wanted to enjoy this trip so for now she would have to let this go.

Jason was hoping that she was not going to back out of the trip. He really screwed this up tonight. He had to figure out how to to make it up to her. He also had to figure out how all this related to him and his lifestyle. This was a simple change he could make. Anna would not like it but they did not travel together all the time anyway. When he got back from the trip he would think about other changes he could make but for now he needed to show Molly he was not a bad guy.

As the train went further up town it started to clear out and they were able to sit down.

"Molly I am truly sorry about tonight."

"I felt like an exhibit in a social experiment. Am I just a charity case to you?"

"No absolutely not."

"Well it sure felt like it, show off the poor cashier to your rich friends. Then you let them chew me up and spit me out."

"I'm really pissed off at Lewis right now. He had no right to judge you and make assumptions."

"Well I guess I did the same with him."

"But it's not the same when you struggle for everything you have and we spend money with no thought of how other people live."

Molly was glad to hear him say that and she softened her attitude a little. She knew their different lifestyles would eventually collide, she just wished it did not have to have been so dramatic. While she was still upset at the situation she still wanted to go on the trip. It was her reward for years of hard work even if it came about in an unconventional way and she still did enjoy Jason's company.

They reached her stop and she guided Jason out to street level. Jason picked up her hand again and as much as she did not want to admit it she could feel the electricity racing up her arm. When they reached her building she turned to him and buried her face in his chest. She stood there breathing in his scent. It had a calming effect on her. It also made her feel safe, wanted and valued especially with the way he had his arms wrapped around her and his head resting on hers.

"This night did not go as I hoped. I wanted to see you again and enjoy a few drinks with friends before I left."

"I know. It's okay."

"No not really."

"Well at least I don't have to see your friends again, but you do." She realized that was probably not the nicest think to say. "I'm sorry, he is your friend."

"No it's okay, he was an ass tonight."

She needed this night to end so she pulled away from him. "Good night Jason. I can't wait for Saturday. Remember A train downtown."

"By the way how are you getting to the airport."

"Train and Katie is coming with me."

"No way, I am arranging for a car service."

"Jason we just talked about this, really I can take the train."

"That's not the point this time. It's going to be really early in the morning and I don't want you on the train then. No arguing I am sending you a car."

She conceded the point. It would save time and be safer. "Okay, thank you. I'm not sure how I'm going to get through the next two days. See you Saturday morning." She hugged him and went inside.

Chapter 7

Molly managed to make it through the last two days of work. Her mind was all over the place from the good times she had with Jason to the tortuous night she endured just two days before. She decided to let her anger go and just focus on the trip. If anything she could explore the island by herself and take advantage of the situation no matter what happened with Jason. At minimum she wanted to stay friendly with him, at least that is what her brain told her. What her heart wanted was entirely different.

As she was triple checking that she had her passport she thought of the kids at her preschool. Today was her last day and she was going to miss them. Some she would see in the elementary school others would move to private schools. She did promise they could always come to her in the future if they needed anything at all. She really hoped that as a teacher she could be a positive role model and make the lives of kids better and give them hope in their own lives.

After she finished packing she was going to Katie's house to have dinner with her family. They were the closet thing to family for her and got her through a lot of tough times. She hoped to do that for others in the future.

The late evening air was heavy with humidity and still very warm. She wondered if it would be the same in St. Lucia. What would the air smell like, would there be a constant breeze, cool at night, would the food be too exotic? She could not wait to try and see everything.

Katie's apartment building was not much different than hers. Not fancy enough for a doorman but filled with respectable hardworking families. She knocked on Katie's family door and was greeted by a woman in her mid fifties. Aunt Rose, which she called Katie's mom, gave her a huge bear hug and ushered her inside. Katie took a deep breath as their apartment always smelled like home cooking. She smiled, "enchiladas?" She loved Aunt Rose's home made enchiladas. They were better than any you could get at a restaurant.

"I know it's your favorite." She smiled at her as they headed for the kitchen. She had spent many evening here over the years. Molly kept to herself in school but Katie had befriended her when she really needed a friend. It was very different from how she grew up. There was always activity here to the point of chaos but there was always plenty of love. And as much as she loved it here she preferred the quietness of her own place.

It was quiet this evening though. Katie was running late from work and her brothers were all out for their Friday night dates. Her brothers treated Molly like another sister either teasing or being over protective. As much as she wanted to see them she was glad they were not there. Tonight she was hoping to get some good advice about her situation with Jason. As much as she loved Katie's go for it attitude she was hoping to get another point of view from someone with a little more experience.

Molly, Rose and her husband Joseph sat at the table and dug into the delicious food. It was eerily quiet. "I'm sorry it's just the three of us," Rose commented.

"I don't mind, actually I wanted to talk to you about something."

Rose patted her lips with her napkin, "you know you can talk to me about anything."

"I know." But she hesitated to go on. She nibbled at her food a little more. She was still struggling with her feelings towards Jason and the situation with Anna and his friends. It really was not even right of her to expect more than a friendship with him. It would be a lot easier if she liked Anna.

Rose, noticing Molly's hesitation, reached out and grabbed her hand. "Honey, tell me what's on your mind."

Before she brought up Jason she was curious about something. "Tell me how you and Uncle Joseph met and how you knew you were in love."

The couple looked at each other and smiled. "I knew from the moment I saw her I was in love with her," Joseph said.

"Except I was more interested in his best friend Anthony."

"Really?" she looked at Joseph, "how did you get her to go out with you?"

"Patience," was his only comment.

"I did date Anthony for a while. Then one day we were all to go out on a double date, I asked a friend to go out with Joseph but neither Anthony or my friend showed up."

"So you two went on the date?"

"Yes we did and here we are still together."

"So how do you know what love feels like?"

"Ah love, it feels like being wrapped in a million tiny bubbles and when they pop it sends tingles all over your body. Sometimes it feels like a warm blanket wrapped around you making you feel safe and secure all the time. You feel like you have wings and can accomplish anything, even fly to the moon. Love does has its up and downs but in the end the person you love is home, your comfort, your best friend and companion. Love is the person you want to share everything with and the person you want to grow old with."

Molly thought about her time with Jason and how he made her feel. The tingle was definitely there and so was the feeling of security. She wanted to tell him more about her life in time and she wanted to know more about him. But was he the one?

"Is this about your trip?" Rose asked her with a knowing smile.

"I really like him Aunt Rose." She felt a twinge of anxiety over her confession but she also felt like a bit of a burden lifted now that she admitted her feelings out loud.

"But . . . ."

"But he has a girlfriend of several years."

"Do you think he likes you?"

"I think he does or at least that is the vibe I get. He pays attention to me, I do things with him when his girlfriend won't. He compliments me all the time."

Aunt Rose smiled at her, "sounds like he is smitten with you. Sounds like you should go for it."

Like mother like daughter Molly smiled inwardly. "And break up his relationship?"

"That is for him to decide not you." She paused thinking more about the situation. "Why do you really think he asked you?"

"I don't know but his girlfriend is a bit of a bitch."

"Maybe he is realizing she is not the one."

Molly would not let herself think that far. There was definitely an attraction going on between them but did it really mean they were meant for each other? "I feel like I am going to get my heart broken if I take this chance."

Joseph responded to this one. "But if you don't take a chance you can't live. Love is always a risk. If you don't take a chance you will never find true love and if you settle you will never find true happiness."

"What if my heart gets broken?"

"Then you tried and you felt love, even if briefly. Then you will continue to live knowing that love is possible."

"Thank you Aunt Rose and Uncle Joseph. I love you guys."

"We love you sweetie," Rose got up to hug her, "go on this trip and have fun, what is meant to be will be. Just one more thing," Rose whispered in her ear, "perhaps fate brought you two together because it is not you that needs this trip, perhaps he is the one that is lost."

Molly held on for a second longer letting that thought roll around in her head. Only time will tell. She headed back to her apartment.

Jason wrapped things up at the office early that day. He planned on making a few stops on his way home then he would make sure he had all his reservations in order. It was a rough few days for him trying to concentrate on wrapping up his work while thinking about his night out with Molly two days ago. He knew he grew up with a certain lifestyle but he never felt so oblivious to everything around him until Molly came along. He also has known Lewis for so long and while he did not agree with all his opinions he never expected such harsh judgement. He hoped Molly thought better of him but then he did not do much to convince her otherwise. At least he would have a week to show her that he did in fact care.

When he entered his apartment he was surprised to see that it was not empty. Anna was in his bedroom with most of her wardrobe spread out across the bed.

"Hey honey, you are home early," Anna greeted him more cheerful than she had been the last few days.

Jason walked over to her and gave her a quick kiss. "I finished early and I had some errands to do. What's going on with the clothes? Did you change your mind about coming with me?" he asked hopefully.

"No, not a chance," she shot him a smug look. "Just trying to figure out what to take to Italy. What do you think of this one?" She asked holding up a long silky dress.

"You know I really like that one," he responded being non committal since she was going to bring what she wanted anyway no matter what he said. "It would look great in the tropics," he added still trying to change her mind. He went to his closet to change out of his work clothes.

"Or in a vineyard in Tuscany."

"I can see that," he conceded but when he returned and really noticed all the clothes on the bed and knowing she had more back at her place it made him think of some of the things Molly said. "I know you want to buy some new clothes in Italy, maybe you won't need to keep all these anymore."

She looked at him as if he asked her to cut off her left arm. "Jason darling you know I need all of these. Clothes for every occasion."

"Surely there must be a few that you could donate."

"Donate? To who?"

"I don't know poor people."

"Are you okay, something going on I need to know about?"

He decided it was a losing argument so he let it go. "No I'm fine, just having thoughts." He wanted to have a nice evening with his long time girlfriend since he would not see her for a week. "As a matter of fact I am having another thought," he looked at her with a big grin.

"Oh yeah what would that be?" she responded seductively.

"That you don't really need clothes at all." he slid her dress straps off her shoulders allowing the dress to fall to the floor.

Anna slid his shirt over his head, "then neither do you."

Chapter 8

Molly was done trying to sleep. She was nervous, anxious but mostly excited. She had everything set to go but made another check, really she only needed her I.D., credit card and passport, surely she could buy anything she missed. She checked the news and weather and washed out her coffee cup to kill some time. She jumped up when there we a knock at her door. Katie was here. She was ecstatic her best friend agreed to accompany her to the airport.

She opened the door with a big grin but Katie did not look real thrilled. "You owe me big time for dragging me out of bed before the sun is up."

"I know, anything you want, thank you for coming."

Katie trudged through the door rubbing her eyes. Molly handed her a thermos of hot coffee. "All ready?" She tried to ask with enthusiasm.

"Yup."

"Dresses, shoes, passport, I.D. money," Molly nodded to each of these things, "condoms."

"Katie!" She gave her friend a light punch, "no way!"

"You never know and you should be prepared," she shrugged back at her.

"No, what if he were to find them?"

"Then he knows what you want."

"Forget it, let's go the car service will be here soon."

"Okay whatever you say, besides men are always prepared" She smiled at her.

Molly had no comment and she really did not want to think about it.

They went outside and only had to wait a few minutes before the car arrived.

"You know I'm really proud of you Molly. I've been bugging you for years to go out and here you at getting on a plane."

"Oh well, I figured I would skip the baby steps and go all out."

"You know I'm actually jealous. When you finish school we need to take a girls trip together."

"Sounds good to me." They talked about potential places for a girls get away. Everything from a weekend getaway to Nantucket to exotic spa trips to Fiji came up. Of course every possibility included massages by gorgeous half naked men. They were having a good time and before they knew it the car was pulling in front of the departure drop off area.

They got out of the car and collected Molly's suitcase. The driver handed Katie a business card with a number to call when she was ready as he would not be allowed to stay in the drop off zone. Jason had said he arranged for the cars to arrive right around the same time. Molly hoped he would not have gone inside without her. She looked around but it was pretty overwhelming to her. She rode the subways all the time but this was different. There were taxis, limos, cars and busses all dropping off passengers. Some people were rushing while others were lingering with their goodbyes. There were men wearing little caps taking people's luggage. She held on tight to hers while watching some of the planes fly low overhead.

"Do you see him?" Katie asked.

Molly looked around again. "No," she replied with an edge of nervousness.

Katie gripped her arm, "don't worry he will show up."

Molly kept watching but honestly it was hard to follow every moving vehicle that stopped to drop people off. She was getting fidgety. In the back of her mind she knew there was a small possibility that he would change his mind but never would let that thought come all the way forward. What would she do if he did not come? Tuck her tail between her legs and go back home she supposed. But if he truly meant to not show up why even send a car for her? She had no way of getting on the plane without him. She pulled out her phone, no message from him so she kept looking.

After a few more anxious minutes Molly caught site of Jason getting out of a car similar to the one that brought her. She grabbed Katie's hand, "he's here." She smiled but was sudden overcome with anxiety. She looked again and saw his beautiful girlfriend stepping out looking absolutely perfect.

Katie followed Molly's gaze and picked out the couple that brought them to this moment. Wow she gave a low whistle, they are a good looking couple.

Molly gave her an icy glare but she knew she was right. She sighed and agreed, "no chance for me then."

"Don't underestimate yourself, especially with your hot new clothes. He is sexy, have fun with him. It's a fantasy trip anyway, don't worry about what happens when you get back."

Molly had plenty of fantasies about Jason but reality was different. She watched the pair head her way, they belonged in a magazine she thought and then remembered that Anna created the magazines. When Jason finally spotted her he held her gaze but showed little emotion. She should not expect too much with Anna by his side.

After the introductions were made Katie pulled Jason aside and started whispering in his ear, then they were fiddling with their phones. Molly could only imagine what she was telling him, hopefully nothing that would embarrass her. Jason kept looking over to her but gave away nothing. Katie had her eyebrow raised meaning she was serious. Molly figured she was probably threatening the wrath of her brothers, for what she was not sure but she was grateful for her friends concerns.

When they turned to come back she saw Anna checking herself out in her compact paying no attention to her or the situation. Neither one attempted to make small talk. Molly was grateful but she also felt small and insignificant around Anna. She knew she should not feel that way and certainly Jason did not make her her feel that way. Jason finally gave her a smile as he got closer and Molly finally felt some of her anxiousness dissipate.

"Well I hate to break up this party but I have to get more beauty sleep before I go to work, I'm going to call for my ride. It was nice meeting you," Katie called to Jason and Anna in an overly cheerful voice.

"I'll meet you inside Jason," Molly wanted a second with Katie alone. When Jason and Anna were out of earshot she asked, "what did you say to him?"

"That you wanted him naked so you could jump his bones as soon as you checked into your room." She smiled at her slyly.

"You did not!" She looked half horrified but knew she was kidding, or hoped so anyway.

"Don't worry about what I said to him, it's all good. My ride is here, have a good trip." The pair hugged and parted ways.

Molly turned and hesitated a half a second. It was her last chance to run away, run back to her simple planned life. She closed her eyes and tried to picture herself on a sandy beach with palm trees. She had to go experience it. Jason or no Jason she focused on the adventure of the island. She took a deep breath and felt her confidence come back. As she went inside she wished she could check in herself and avoid Anna but it would only be a few more minutes.

The inside was just as busy as the outside so when she located Jason she stuck close to him. As they headed to the airline desk she grimaced at the long line but Jason confidently walked over to the priority access area where there was no one waiting. He looked at Molly, "advantage of being frequent fliers."

She just nodded, there were so many things she wanted to know but did not want to look any more ignorant that she was. They showed their I.D.'s, had their luggage weighed and tagged and were given boarding passes.

"Last chance Anna, please come." Jason actually sounded a little desperate.

"What about her?" Anna nodded towards Molly.

"I'll buy another ticket, reserve another room."

"You would do that?"

"Yes, if you change your mind right now, we can buy everything you need when we get there."

Molly was listening and starting to panic, this was not what she imagined. There was no way she could last a week watching them together. The best she could hope was the resort was big enough for the three of them. She did know she could not stand and listen to this conversation even though Anna did not appear to be swayed and it was awkward.

"I thought you enjoyed our vacations together."

"I do, of course I do, I just don't want to go to the beach."

"But you would look sexy in a bikini." he stepped towards her wrapping his warms around her shoulders.

"Yes," she practically purred at him but quickly changed her tone, "until sweat starts dripping down my head ruining my make up."

That was about as much as Molly could take. "Uh hey, Jason, if you don't mind I'll take my boarding pass and meet you by the gate."

"Are you sure?" he asked but did not take his eyes off Anna.

"Yeah it's fine, we seem to be really early anyway. I can figure out where to go."

"Okay, I'll be there soon, call me if you have any problems." He handed Molly the pass but stayed partly attached to Anna.

She took the pass and left them. She was glad to be away from that conversation. Of course she should expect that they would be physically intimate. They had been together for some time. She had to separate her feelings for Jason from this trip. Surely she could find other single men to hang with once they got there. Yes, that is what she would do. Feeling better about life she looked around to find the way to her gate. She got through most of life by herself surely she could handle the airport. She smiled to herself, her vacation was starting. She wanted to take it all in. She could not believe all the shops and restaurants, it was like being in an upscale mall. As much as she wanted to stop and browse she really wanted to make it to the boarding area then maybe she would look around.

She made her way to the security checkpoint. There was a long line but she was glad in a way as she could watch to see what everyone else was doing. She tossed her purse and her shoes in a bucket and waited to be waived through the x-ray machine. Through with no trouble she breathed a sigh of relief. Not that she had anything to hide of course but being alone going through the first time was nerve wracking.

She followed the signs to the gate. She was early and there were only a few people there. No one was at the desk but the sign read St. Lucia. She took out her phone and snapped a picture then sent it to Katie. If she wasn't an adult she would jump for joy so instead she smiled and looked around. She had already been up for a while so she went to the coffee stand for an orange juice and pastry. She found a seat by the window so she could see what was happening outside. It was like a well orchestrated play with vehicles going in all different directions. She got to watch the luggage being loaded and unloaded. The planes were pushed back by heavy duty vehicles. It was all so amazing to her and she could not take her eyes off the activity.

She was not sure how much time had passed when there as a thump by her feet. She looked over to see Jason flopping down in the seat next to her. He leaned forward with fists and jaw clenched. The silence was too much.

"Are you okay."

"Fine."

"You don't look fine." No response. He came alone but she had to know for sure. "I guess she's not coming then?"

"She's not here is she?" he asked with more that a slight edge of sarcasm.

While she did feel somewhat bad for him she was also relieved but this was not starting off well and it was bringing her mood down. "Well if you are going to be in a bad mood you can go sit somewhere else. I'm trying to enjoy myself."

He looked at her but neither responded nor moved. She looked back at him and tried to lighten his mood. "Well I know what your real problem is anyway."

That got him, "oh yeah and what would that be?"

She pulled out her phone and showed him the picture of the St. Lucia sign.

"I know where we are going, what's your point?"

"Well I think, of course I have not been there," she shrugged, "but I do believe it is hot there. And here you are in socks, heavy loafers, long pants and a long sleeve shirt. Can you even breathe in that?"

Apparently he could not breathe since he did still did not respond. She sighed, "why don't you go for a walk and blow off some steam."

He picked up his bag and walked off. Who was she to criticize his clothes? Didn't she say Katie helped her shop. So what if Anna picked out his clothes on occasion, okay maybe frequently. Eventually he came across a men's upscale clothing store and he went inside. He felt bad he treated Molly rudely. The argument with Anna was not her fault or her problem. He started to relax and when he did he realized he was in fact getting hot in his outfit. He tried to concentrate on the clothes but he was not sure what he did like. He did not understand why this was so hard, he made important decisions at work all the time but for this he was clueless.

He left and went to a shoe store. This seemed a little easier. At least he could gear it towards the necessity of the trip. He picked out leather strap sandals and wore them out of the store. He found a more casual clothing store and felt more comfortable.

He picked out a pair of cargo type shorts and a fitted v neck t-shirt. He stopped at the men's room to change. He left his shoes and outfit purposely in the bathroom. He headed back to Molly feeling much better.

He sat back down next to her. "I'm sorry for being rude. I do feel better."

Molly looked and him and appreciated the way his t shirt showed off his muscles. She felt flushed but could not take her eyes off him. It was going to take a very good looking man to distract her from Jason. She looked in eyes and said, "you look good but it needs one more thing."

"Really?" he asked almost pouting, he thought he chose well.

She laughed and ran her hand through his head ruffling his perfectly combed hair.

"There that is better."

The brief head massage felt real good and he did not want her stop. Instead he took her hand in his and started with his soothing massage. That sense of peace it gave came back again. "I'm sorry again, can we start over?"

She squeezed his hand. "Stop apologizing. Actually I would be upset too if I was in your situation." She unwillingly let go of his hand, she felt it was inappropriate. He looked sort of sad and she felt bad for him so she picked up his hand again and returned the favor of the massage. She hoped the good tingles she felt would never go away and she hoped he was feeling it also. She wondered what she would feel if their lips ever met. The thought was heating her up too much. She could not imagine any other man that would cause her to push Jason aside. If nothing else she could enjoy his company but for now talking seemed safer. It kept her emotions in check. Emotions that she knew may not be reciprocated. "This place is amazing. Crazy too, but really fascinating."

"Yeah I guess." He answered looking a little confused.

"I know most people see it as a way to get from point a to b but to me it is a place of hope."

"Hope? Not when the lines are long, security picks you to be searched, your flight is delayed and you luggage is lost."

"Hmm, of course I have no experience with such things. I meant hope for what is to come. I hope to have a great vacation. I hope I land that business deal. I hope to make it on Broadway. I would think everyone is hoping for something no matter where they are going."

"So what is your hope for this trip?"

"Me? I hope I can let go a little, not control every moment. I hope I can be adventurous and try new things. Which I have already done, this airport is an adventure in itself." She laughed then added softly, "I hope I can feel," but she was not ready to elaborate. "What about you, what would you hope for on this trip?" she quickly turned the tables on him.

"I hope you have a fantastic trip." He gave that obvious answer only because he was no longer sure what he wanted. He remembered when he was planning this trip. There was a purpose. And while he did get a good deal there was something else he had been planning. He was not sure if he should share it with Molly but he felt comfortable with her and he really just needed to talk to someone. He reached into his backpack and pulled out a small box. "Actually I did hope for something when I planned this trip."

Molly gasped when she saw the little blue box with the white ribbon. Every woman knew what that was, the little blue box from Tiffany's. She knew it was not for her but just seeing one up close would have an affect on anyone. She did wonder though if this meant there was no chance with Jason anymore, would he propose in Italy? Well the ring was not on Anna's finger yet.

"You were going to propose to Anna?" She asked nonchalantly.

"That was the plan," he said in a far away voice. "I imagined a beautiful sunset, just the two of us on the beach, or something like that."

Molly closed her eyes picturing herself at that moment. Then she realized he said that was the plan. Was, that word changed things in her mind. "And that is why you were so upset she did not come?"

"Partly." He looked at Molly, "open it tell me what you think."

"No I couldn't."

He opened it instead and pulled out a dazzling square cut two carrot diamond set in platinum. Molly took it and pretended to inspect it like a professional then put it on her ring finger and held her hand out in front of them. "Well its okay if you like this sort of style." She continued to look at it. What she really felt was far different. First she never had seen anything that sparkled so brilliantly. Also she had nothing in her personal possession that costs anywhere near what this must have. She kept staring in awe at its beauty. She should give it back, in another minute, it was nice to dream.

Jason watched her pretending not to think much of the ring. He knew it was a high quality diamond, there would be nothing less for the woman he would marry. She was hiding her emotions pretty well, he could tell that she was awed by it. It was not her style and pictured something more fine and delicate on her finger. He knew which one it would be. He had seen one at Tiffany's but it had not been right for Anna. He wished he could shake this confusion, he should not be looking at one ring thinking about a ring for someone else.

He sighed thinking about his confusion and then thinking about how Molly also hides her emotions. Maybe not about him. He liked her innocence and the way she shyly flirted with him. He knew she liked him but was guarded because of Anna. There were other things in her life that kept her guarded in general and he wanted to know more. "So what did you mean by you wanted to feel again?"

She kept looking at the ring, purposely avoiding his eyes thinking she was impressed that he did hear what she said. "You know sand, palm trees, ocean water." She was still trying to keep things casual. She took the ring off her finger and handed it back. "It's really beautiful, I am sure she is going to love it." She bit her lip and turned away from him.

He took the ring back and placed it back in the box. He pulled out another larger box and put it in her lap since she was not looking his way. "I got something for you."

Perhaps showing her the ring had not been the best idea especially since he did know of her feelings for him. He was just so frustrated with the situation he really just wanted to talk about it. And now it was out in the open although it did not resolve anything. He hoped this gift to her would bring her cheery mood back.

Molly looked at the package. She felt on the verge of tears. There had not been many presents in her life. "You did not have to get me anything, the trip is enough."

"Open it."

She unwrapped the box in anxious anticipation and almost squealed when she saw what it was. He got her a digital camera, another thing she never owned. She turned to him and wrapped both arms around him. She held on to him and breathed in his scent. Somehow he always knew what she needed and understood that she was not an extravagant person. She whispered in his ear. "I love it, thank you." When she let go of him she added, "besides this is way better than the silly little ring in the little blue box."

He felt a rush of warmth and appreciation. It gave him great joy to see her reactions, not only to a simple gift but to everything they have done together so far. "It's all set up and ready to use. The battery is charged and new memory card installed."

She took the shiny pink camera out of the box and turned it on. "Good color choice."

Just then another passenger was walking by, Molly stood up and asked the woman to take a picture of the two of them. She wanted the very first picture to be a treasured memory. Jason stood up behind her and wrapped his arms around the front of her. He tucked his head down next to hers and she leaned into him.

She felt like he was the perfect fit for her and smiled for the picture.

The woman took the picture and smiled. "You two make a lovely couple." But as she handed the camera back her eyes became distant. "Your auras are blending to make beautiful colors." The she snapped back and looked into Molly's eyes. "And Julie approves."

Molly could not believe her ears. The color drained away from her face and she fell back into the chair.

Jason was confused and concerned about her reaction. "Molly what's wrong, who is Julie?" Jason wanted to stop the lady but she was oddly gone.

Molly was trembling but she managed to reply. "Julie is my sister."

"Do you know her, does she know your sister?" He looked again for the lady but did not see her so he knelt down in front of Molly and held her hands.

Molly faced him glassy eyed, "my sister died over ten years ago."

Jason swallowed hard, he had no idea how to respond. He never knew what to believe when it came to auras and spirits. Just then there was an announcement that boarding would begin shortly. He helped her up and wrapped his arms around her again. He asked if she was okay as he ran his hand through her long soft hair. He felt a twinge of guilt knowing that she was distressed but being so close to her caused a rush of pleasure that was coursing through his body.

Molly felt his warmth and her breathing settled and her hands stopped shaking. Maybe it was coincidence or the lady was crazy or she did not know what. She always did feel that Julie was watching after her. That thought and Jason's warmth gave her strength and put her mind back in the moment.

She stepped back and squeezed his strong hands. "I'm good, thanks. I'm ready to go."

They walked over to the boarding entrance. "But watch out I'm going to be one of those crazy ladies taking pictures of everything." She smiled and pointed the camera in his direction.

He just laughed as they joined the line for priority access. He was glad she seemed to gain her color back. He was going to ask about her sister though and he hoped she would open up to him.

Chapter 9

"So what's the big deal about boarding first since we all have assigned seats?" She felt better asking questions without Anna, experienced traveller, around.

"Well more people are taking luggage on board so there is less space in the overhead bins. It's nice to be settled in while everyone is boarding. Anyhow it comes with my frequent flier status and the line is shorter so I use it."

Molly took it all in as they headed into the gangway that took them to the plane. She touched the outside of the plane. She wanted to feel the machine that would take them thousands of feet in the air, give it a little good luck pat as well. She stepped inside and saw the cockpit. She wanted to go in and look at all the little lights and switches but knew she had to keep moving. She also noticed the circulating air that had an odd scent like nothing she ever smelled but would

Lesley Esposito

always associate with airplanes. They walked past the large leather seats and she assumed this was first class. She looked back at Jason, "do you ever fly first class?"

"On occasion." They reached their coach seats and he gestured for her to take the window seat. He put his backpack in the overhead bin and grabbed a pillow and blanket for Molly.

"Thanks," she replied even though it was pretty warm on the plane. "How long will it be before we take off?"

"Not long, as soon as everyone is on and seated we should head out to the runway. Are you nervous?"

"A little but mostly excited." She looked out the window and watched the luggage being put on board. She was still fascinated by the fact that her luggage went from the check in all the way to the plane, well at least she hoped it did. Before she knew it the flight attendants were doing their final check and they were heading to the runway. She watched the safety video and took in all the details. She always liked to be prepared. Of course she did not want to think of the implications but it was good to know what to do.

The plane turned and the pilot announced they were cleared for takeoff. Molly grabbed Jason's hand and held on tight as she looked out the window. As the plane picked up speed she felt her weight being pulled back in the seat and she squeezed his hand even harder.

The plane lifted in the air and she was pushed down into her seat. She continued looking out the window as the plane then tilted. It was very disorientating for her and a little nerve wracking. Finally they leveled out as they continued their ascent. She eased her grip, "that was intense."

"Keep looking, you should be able to see the city."

"The skyline is amazing from up here, the cars look like toys."

"I picked our seats on this side of the plane so you can watch the coastline as we fly south."

She watched everything shrink, the houses, shopping centers, and roadways. Some spots had so many trees it looked like forests but then there were the open fields of the farms that took on all different shapes and colors. Then she saw the ocean and marveled at its blueness. The sky was also clear and you could see forever. She felt like she could stare out this window the entire four hour flight.

She finally did turn her attention back to the plane. She looked at what was in the seat pouch in front of her. She pulled out the little paper bag, "do people actually throw up on planes?"

"Sometimes I guess."

"Yuck." She pulled out the Sky Mall catalog. It was filled with a lot of interesting gadgets. She flipped through it and asked, "so what do you typically do when you fly?"

"Sometimes work, sleep, watch a movie, listen to music."

"Hmm, what about Anna?"

"Mostly sleeps or reads a magazine."

She put the catalog back and looked back out the window. They were further out over the ocean but she could still see the sandy beaches. There were also some low lying clouds far below. It made her think of rainy days and how the clouds were closer to the ground than she thought.

The drink cart came through and Jason ordered mimosas for both of them. He toasted her, "to a trip full of hope."

They clinked cups and she she sipped the cocktail. The bubbles tickled her tongue and she felt the drink send warmth through her nervous system. After a few more sips she felt her body relax. She decided to use their time in the air to get to know more about Jason.

"So tell me about your childhood."

"I guess it was a typical suburban upbringing, school, friends and sports." He did leave out the part of the oversized house in the gated community, custom pool and pool house in the backyard. He wanted to downplay their differences.

"What did you play?"

"Baseball, outfield."

"Did you ever aspire to be a professional player?"

"No, I wasn't that good, decent but not that good. Anyway you know I was pretty destined to go into finance."

"What about family, do you have lots of relatives and big gatherings?"

"Just a few cousins but my parents loved to entertain especially in the summer. They have a great yard with decks, a pool and clubhouse." he paused realizing he overstepped what he planned to say but he had a good childhood and he was just excited to share it with her. "My my mom was always in charge. She always had the dinner catered but she made her own desserts. My friends and I were always the taste testers. It was a good thing we were active otherwise we would have all been fifty pounds overweight." He chuckled at the memory.

Molly was smiling at him but there was a wistful look in her eyes. He hoped she was willing to open up to him. Something happened in her past. He hoped she would tell him so he could make it right. He reached down and pulled her feet onto his lap. He pulled off her shoes. She went with it and turned to lean sideways in her seat facing him. He started rubbing her feet. "Will you tell me about Julie?" he asked her softly.

She lowered her eyelids but did not look away. "To tell you about Julie is to tell you my life story."

He did not respond, just kept rubbing her feet. She could feel him looking into her soul again waiting for her to open the window into her past. There were only a handful of people who knew how she grew up. She decided to take a chance and tell him even though it would be difficult but it was the only way he would fully understand her and who she was and is now.

She looked back in his eyes, "I will tell you but I only ask that you do not interrupt." He gave a slight nod and she looked past him and searched out her memories.

She was back in her tiny two bedroom basement apartment. It was always dark, musty and smelled of smoke but it was her home. Her mother had fiery red hair with, at one time, the personality to match. When she graduated high school she planned on making it on Broadway. She got a few bit parts but never stayed with them too long, she wanted to be the star. One night she met Molly's father, he was a handsome Italian who promised her connections to producers. They partied hard and by the time she figured out there were no leads she found out she was pregnant.

Her parents moved in together and they had Molly. At first her mother tried to do the right thing. She stopped smoking and cut back on the drinking. She worked whatever odd jobs she could find. Her father was not around much. He stayed out late and slept late. Molly always had to be quiet when he was home so her mother took her to the park then they would go home and she would tell her bedtime stories. But it was not long before her mother became depressed and started drinking again. Molly was often left with a neighbor or the building supervisor and her parents started going out together late into the night. By the time Molly was five her mother was pregnant again.

She knew her father was angry and to please him her mother kept up with the partying. She made an effort to cut out the drinking but it was too late, she was already an alcoholic and was unable to stop. Julie was born with fetal alcohol syndrome. Their mother was sent to rehab in order to take the baby home. She made her promises to stop and they were released from the hospital.

Little Julie was a handful though. She cried all the time and it pissed off her father. Molly was extremely protective of her sister and was constantly consoling her. She learned to change her diapers and feed her but she was also starting school. She would always run home and as soon as she walked in the door her mother would hand her over. Her depression grew and her father became even angrier and finally left when Julie turned one.

Molly took a breather. She kept her eyes closed not wanting to see the reaction on Jason's face. She could feel the tension rise and fall as the pressure of her foot massage changed. If she looked at him she would probably have a melt down and she wanted to finish her story.

Molly begged her mother to let her stay home without a babysitter. She started watching cooking shows and learned how to cook basic meals. Her mother would buy what they needed and there was always a plate of food waiting when she got home from work. She also learned that certain foods affected her sister more than others.

The next few years were actually pretty good for the sisters. They had freedom and a routine. Most afternoons were spent outdoors no matter the weather. Julie loved rain and snow and they stayed out until the sun went down. When they couldn't be out they went to the library and rented books and videos. Julie loved anything with princesses and Molly read her fairy tales every night.

Halloween was their favorite holiday. Every year they cut eyes holes out of sheets and raced around as ghosts. They collected as much candy as fast as they could and would go crazy for one night. After that Molly would have to hide the candy and portion it out otherwise Julie would go crazy from sugar highs.

When Julie started school life got a little harder. Julie had a short attention span and was having trouble but Molly spent every day between going outside and doing homework. She also got sick a lot being exposed to all the other kids. It seemed she did not have a strong immune system. There were days Molly would have to stay home with her. But through it all they still had a strong bond and were inseparable.

Julie was sick and it was the middle of winter when Molly thought her sister was getting another cold. She fed her the usual chicken soup and kept her fever down but she was having trouble breaking it. She got up for school and she seemed so weak. Her mother promised to take her to the doctor but when she came home her mother was asleep and Julie was burning up. She put her in a cold tub and she seemed to be better but the next morning she had broken out in a rash and her breathing was shallow and raspy. She could not wake her mother either but that was the empty vodka bottle. Molly took money out of her mothers purse and got a cab to take her and her sister to the hospital.

She was quickly admitted and placed in isolation. It turned out she had the measles. They did not want Molly to be with her but she argued she was already exposed and refused to leave. They hooked Julie up to machines and fluids but because her immune system was so weak she could not fight it. She died that night with Molly by her side.

Molly was suddenly aware that Jason had stopped rubbing her feet. She had to keep going though and let it all out and get to the point where they were now.

It was crazy that next day. Molly had a mild case of the measles but did not have to be hospitalized. Then they vaccinated her with everything she should have had, she felt like a pin cushion. Social services came out to her house. She forced her mother to stay sober enough to get through the inspections. As angry as she was she did not want to lose the only home she ever had. After a few home visits they were left alone.

That spring Molly met Katie and they became fast friends. Molly spent a lot of time with Katie's family and they helped her through her anger and depression. She missed Julie so much and she struggled with her emotions towards her mother. She did learn that there were families that loved and supported each other, families where parents were home for dinner and they did things all together. This is what she wanted and she made a decision to get out of her situation. Katie's mother helped her get her job at the supermarket. Even though she was underage she was paid off the books for the first year.

For two years Molly worked and saved every penny she earned. One day she came home and there was an eviction notice on her door. She assumed her mother was working since there was still food in the house and her mother came and went at the same times every day. She walked in to see her mother passed out he again. All the anger came flooding back. She took her money and went to her landlord. She paid the back rent and begged him to let her stay promising to pay the rent and begging him not not raise the price. He had sympathy for her and let her stay. When she went back she packed up her mothers things and kicked her out. She had the locks changed and told her to never come back.

"Ever since then I have been working and going to school. Katie's mom helped me get scholarships and as you know I graduate in December. It's been hard but it's almost over. Then one day I randomly met you and here we are."

She finally had the nerve to look at Jason. When their eyes met she saw a range of emotions from anger to sadness. "It's okay Jason. I don't want you to be angry and I don't want a bunch of sympathy. I am happy with where I am in my life. I have moved on and plan to keep moving on. There are a lot things I plan on doing once I graduate. This is why this trip is so special to me and it's only the beginning for me and I know Julie is in a happy place and she is now watching out for me."

Molly looked out the window again and suddenly felt very tired. It was like a heavy weight had been lifted. It had been a long day and she leaned back against the pillow and closed her eyes. She fell asleep within minutes.

Jason watched her angelic face. A peacefulness had settled on her. He was a mixed bag of emotions. He was angry about what happened in her life. He wanted to yell at someone, how could they let this happen? She was right that he lived in a far more insulated world than she did. He was glad for Katie and her family, he understood why her best friend was so protective of her. Molly was so strong now, she knew what she wanted and was going after it. He almost felt helpless, he wanted to do something for her. He studied her face again and he understood that he was doing what she needed. She just needed a companion, someone to experience new things with. He could do that, show her the world, show her beauty, life, trust and maybe more.

Two hours later Molly stirred and stretched. She opened her eyes to find Jason smiling at her. She smiled back. "I guess I was tired. I was too excited to sleep much last night."

"Its okay, I'm glad you got some rest." He let go of her legs and she stretched as much as she could. "And I want to thank you for sharing your sister with me. I know it was difficult."

And she was ready to put the memories back to rest again, it was time to move on. "You're welcome." She smiled and thanked him with her eyes gazing into his. She looked out the window to see endless blue ocean but then she realized, "I need to use the bathroom."

Jason got up to let her out, "remember to lock the door and don't get flushed out, its a long way down," he said as he winked at her.

A few minutes later she returned. "You weren't kidding about that flushing thing, that toilet will suck you in if you're not careful. And I'm glad we are not sitting back there, it's loud and bouncy."

As she sat down the pilot announced they would be landing in twenty minutes. Molly looked back out the window and could see a small island out in the distance. She kept her eyes glued and watched as it grew in size. They started descending and Molly could feel her stomach rising. This was not her favorite part of the flight. She leaned back, closed her eyes and grabbed Jason's hand. She could hear the engines shifting and the wing flaps coming down. She took a few deep breaths. Jason leaned over her to look out the window. His face was so close to hers and she felt the warmth of his breath. It calmed her in a way but she also felt flush. She wanted to reach over and kiss him but thought that with her luck the plane would bounce and they would clunk heads.

Jason was having the same thought. He looked at her sweet pink lips and wanted to taste them, but then the plane did jolt and he sat back in his seat. "Are you ready?"

"Do I have a choice?" She asked a little shaky.

"We'll be down in a minute."

The plane touched down with a slight bounce. Molly was pulled forward as she could suddenly feel the speed. She managed to glance outside to see the scenery rushing by and before she knew it they were rolling along heading to the terminal. She couldn't wait to get outside.

Chapter 10

The plane stopped and all the passengers stood up. She was a little confused since they were still a slight distance from the terminal. "No portable hallway thing?"

"No, at these smaller airports sometimes you have to walk across the tarmac."

"Oh," she grabbed her purse and stepped in front of Jason in the aisle. When she exited the plane she stopped briefly at the top of the stairs. She took a deep breath. The air was warm and humid but there was a breeze blowing as well. She could see green mountains in the distance and swaying palm trees not too far away. She wanted to run and immerse herself in the landscape.

They crossed the hot asphalt and headed into the small airport. The rush of cool air was quite a contrast to the hot, humid air outside. They followed the signs to go through customs. After she had her passport stamped she had Jason take a picture with her showing off her first stamp. She hoped there would be a lot more in her future.

After fetching their luggage they headed over to ground transportation. Jason explained that the hotel would be picking them up and he had not planned on renting a car hoping to spend more time on the beach and that they could use the busses if needed. Molly had no problem with that but she was somewhat surprised since Jason seemed to have an issue with public transportation.

The ride was about an hour and just like on the plane Molly was glued to the changing scenery. The foliage was amazing, the leaves on the trees were huge and there were flowers blooming everywhere. They passed small shacks, food vendors and huge mansions as they wove their way through the mountains. It was a little scary as well, there did not seem to be anything to prevent them from careening off the mountain side.

"Hey look, did you know bananas grow upside down?" She asked Jason excitedly but kept her attention outside.

He chuckled but actually he did not know that. He was really enjoying watching her take in everything for the first time. It also helped him to really see things he normally would not have paid any attention to.

"You said you had plans for after school, what else were you looking forward to doing?"

Molly turned to him. "Well after I figure out my finances I plan on taking in some Broadway shows, last minute half price tickets of course."

"What about traveling?"

"I have my passport but I definitely want to see more of our country. California, Yosemite, Florida, Grand Canyon all top my list."

Jason could imagine taking these trips as well, sightseeing and adventure instead of shopping. He hoped they could do some of that here as well.

After stopping at several other hotels they reached their resort. They gathered their luggage and headed to the check in area. It was an open air reception area and they were all greeted by the friendly staff and were offered cocktails. Molly took one of the fruity drinks and let Jason handle the check in process. She walked around appreciating the huge flower arrangements and lush seating. She found a rack of brochures for all the different activities on the island. She took one of everything planning on looking through them later on once they were settled in.

After Jason got their room key they were led to a large golf cart and were driven to their room. Molly took a few pictures along the way, she was a little nervous about the room arrangements since it was not originally intended for her. Jason showed her how to use the room key so that she could go in first. The room was washed in a variety of blues with white trims and furnishings. There were light orange accents, tiled floors and ceiling fans. She walked around the room touching everything taking in its simple beauty. She did note that there was a small couch and one king size bed.

"I can sleep on the couch," Jason said sort of reading her mind.

"The couch is kind of small, I'm sure we can manage on the bed, maybe put a line of pillows down the middle." She would worry about that later. She headed towards the french doors and opened them up. They were on the ground floor so they had a small patio with a table and two chairs. There was a grassy area that was lined by rocks and the ocean water was softly lapping against the rocks. There were coconut palms framing the whole scene. It was the most incredible thing Molly had ever seen.

She sat down on the grass and let the warm ocean breeze envelope her. This place was magical, no wonder people came here to do their soul searching. Her eyes were glistening when Jason sat down next to her.

He noticed the tear starting to form and was suddenly concerned. He pushed her hair back but let his hand stay resting on her head. "Everything okay?" he asked softly.

"It's so beautiful. You can see pictures and dream about what it would be like but there is no comparison to actually being here."

He almost turned to kiss her but he felt it would disrupt her moment of serenity. As much as wanted to stay with her he felt it was her hard earned moment. He stood up and told her he was going inside to unpack.

She was not sure how he understood her need to be alone but she appreciated it. She sat watching the rays of the sun dance on the water. The ocean changed colors with each passing cloud. The scene was mesmerizing. There were a few sailboats out in the distance adding to the perfection. She heard the leaves of the palms rustle in the wind. She wanted to get up and hug the tree but thought that might look odd so she took a few more photos instead. She shot wide angle and a bunch of close ups focusing on color and textures. It was inspiring her to redecorate her apartment.

Somewhat reluctantly, but she knew she had all week to soak in the scenery, she got up and went inside their room. She planned to unpack then shower before dinner. She laughed when she saw Jason flinging all his clothes all over the couch. "What's going on?"

"I did not pack these clothes," he pointed to his mess. "Now I know why she did not want to go out the other night. I was packing and she said she did not feel well. She replaced my clothes while I was gone.

This sucks, I'm not wearing any of this." He picked up the whole pile and dumped it back in his suitcase.

"Wow," Molly responded a little stunned. "I guess we will have to go shopping after all."

"Great," he responding still huffing.

"Or you can walk around in just your bathing suit all week." That would be a sight she could live with.

He gave no response as he went about huffing and stuffing his suitcase in the closet.

Molly ignored him and went about the business of putting her clothes in drawers and hanging her dresses. When she was finished she brought her toiletries into the bathroom and told Jason she was taking a shower. The water pressure was strong and she lingered under the hot stream longer than she normally does. Instead of blow drying her hair she put it up in a loose bun and applied the little bit of make up Katie showed her.

Jason took her spot in the bathroom while she slipped on her dress and sandals. She went outside to wait for him while she watched the sun lowering towards the horizon. She was a little nervous. This dress was meant to get his attention. She knew he came close to kissing her several times. She wanted him to make the first move, let him make the decision but she smiled and thought she could certainly encourage him.

He finished showering and put the same shorts back on. His phone rang and he ignored it. He found a shirt he could live with but he refused to tuck it in. He needed to relax and settle into this trip. They only just got here and did not think he could handle these intense swings of emotions. One minute he was so drawn to Molly, then next he was fuming at Anna but he also meant to propose marriage to her. Where was Molly anyway? The patio door was open and he went out to find her.

What he saw stopped him in his tracks. She was standing facing the ocean wearing a long flowing dress. The back scooped just below her waistline showing off her creamy skin from her neck down. He was so heated he felt like his shoes would melt to the ground. He needed to feel her silkiness, inhale her scent and to taste her sweetness.

Molly could feel him watching her. She was frozen with anticipation. She felt his warmth breath on her neck. She broke out in goosebumps that sent a shiver through her whole body. She actually shook slightly when he started tracing the outline of her dress with his finger. She heard his phone ring and she froze but quickly relaxed when he ignored it.

"You are stunning. And you are definitely flirting with me."

She melted with his words and his touch. She smiled and turned to face him. She saw the intensity in his eyes as they studied her. When his gaze lowered to her lips she closed her eyes. He rubbed his finger over her lips and she parted them slightly waiting.

The phone rang inside their room and the sound made her jump back. She laughed and said, "someone really wants to talk to you."

"Don't move," he said with a low growl.

She watched him go in trying to catch her breath. She watched him talking into the phone trying to decipher what was going on. He started pacing as far as the phone cord would allow him to go. Molly stepped a little closer but stopped at the edge of the patio. She could hear his voice raising. After listening for a minute she realized he was having an argument with Anna. It seemed she could not actually believe that he went on the trip anymore than he couldn't believe she would not go. When he started in about the clothes Molly decided she did not want to hear anymore so she turned and headed over to the restaurant by herself.

The restaurant was a large open air building shaped like a circular hut complete with thatch roofs and ceiling fans. There were several buffet tables filled with a huge variety of food with open seating. Molly looked around, she did not particularly want to sit by herself. She spotted another lone diner, he appeared to be in his thirties, very athletic but a little stiff military looking. He seemed safe so she approached him with a smile. After all, this was part of her experience. She was trying to meet new people. "Hi, are you here by yourself? Can I sit with you?"

"Yes, and absolutely," he stood up and pulled put a chair for her but also gave her a whole body glance over. "I'm Paul," he offered his hand.

Well at least he is polite with good manners even if he was looking her up and down, Molly thought to herself. "Molly," she shook his hand, "the food looks fabulous, any recommendations?"'

"The seafood is fresh and delicious."

"Well I'm starving so if you don't mind I'm going to fill up a plate."

"No problem, can I get you something from the bar?"

"Sure, something fruity and tropical?"

Trying to stick with the be adventurous theme Molly piled her plate with food she never tried although some of the shell fish she was not even sure how to eat so she passed on those for now. After adding salad she headed back to the table where Paul was waiting with a white frosty drink.

"Mai tai," he slid the glass over.

"Thank you," she took a sip of the coconut drink and first felt the cold but then a warming from the alcohol. She would have to be careful not to drink too many.

After a few bites of her dinner she decided to try this make polite conversation with a stranger idea. "So Paul, why are you here by yourself?"

"Post divorce celebration," he added a smile and chuckle.

"Hmm, celebration? Well then congratulations. How long we're you married?"

"Ten years." There was a slight sadness to his voice.

"Any kids?"

"No but my wife, excuse me, ex-wife claims the kids on the football team are my kids. I do spend a lot of time with them. It's my passion to make them great players but also to make them the best person they can be on and off the field." He beamed with pride.

"Did you want kids of your own?"

"I did but I guess we grew too far apart."

"What level do you coach?"

"High school, plus I'm a history teacher. I love the Civil War and Southern history."

Molly was excited and told him about her plans to be a teacher. He gave her some advice on being a new teacher and she shared some new ideas she had learned in school. She was glad she sat with Paul. She thought she needed to stop making up stories about people and start talking to them more. Although sometimes she would still need a way to entertain and amuse herself.

"So what about you?" Paul asked changing the course of the conversation, "some how I don't think you are here by yourself."

"No, not exactly," she replied with eyes lowered.

"Well, then I say he is fool letting you out by yourself, especially dressed like that." He leaned towards her with a smile as he said that. "There are plenty of single men here and there is not one that has not noticed you."

Molly blushed at the compliment. She did notice a few glances her way but she was still not totally comfortable with the attention.

"So who is this guy?"

Molly was a little surprised at how insightful Paul was but maybe the situation was more obvious then she thought. She told him the short story version of how she came to be on the island. "When I left him he was having an argument with his girlfriend, practically fiancé," she added with a hint of sarcasm.

Paul gazed at her silently for a minute then responded. "I can tell you magic happens on these islands, that is why people come here. Let the magic work, if it is meant to be then it will happen."

"So what magic are you seeking?"

"The one that erases the image of my wife, sorry ex wife, with another man. Looking at you I think it is starting to work."

Molly smiled at him. He was good looking but she did not feel the same spark as when Jason looked at her or touched her. Paul was still good company and she was glad to have met him.

"There is a steel drum band playing at the lounge tonight, shall we go over and check it out."

Molly scanned around the room and did not spot Jason, oh well, his loss. "I would love to."

They stopped at the bar to grab another round of drinks then found a table in the lounge area. There was a small stage with a dance floor in front of it and tables set randomly around the open area. There was a local band playing a mixture of reggae and steel drum music. There were a few couples moving around the dance floor. The hotel photographer was buzzing around catching memories. Molly was sipping her drink letting it warm her insides and calm her nerves.

"Do you want to dance?" Paul asked.

"I'm not very good."

"Well that makes two of us," Paul stood up and offered his hand.

Their dancing started out awkwardly but soon they let loose and stomped and swayed around the floor. They were laughing and making fun of themselves. They posed for the photographer pretending to be a giddy couple in love.

Molly was not sure how much time went by when Paul whispered in her ear, "I think your man is here." She tensed up slightly but wondered how Paul knew since she had never described Jason to him.

"Really, how do you know?"

"There's a guy at the bar watching you, but he's staring me down."

Molly turned to see Jason sitting on the stool, eyes squinted, eyebrows pressed together. "He looks mad."

"Oh yeah, he's pissed off all right. And that only means one thing."

"What's that?" Molly asked pulling Paul closer into another spin

"He is jealous and he wants you bad!"

"Well if he wants me, he can come and get me," she grinned stepping even closer to her dance partner.

She was taunting him, and doing it on purpose. Jason could feel himself tensing. He had his eye on Molly and that guy the whole time. The guy knew it too and for a while. He was keeping Molly from looking in his direction. They were obviously enjoying each others company, a little too much in his opinion. When her new friend finally decided to alert her to his presence he could not believe she had the nerve to step in closer. He was jealous for sure and he could not bear to watch them any longer.

He weaved his way through the couples and tapped Molly on the shoulder. "May I cut in?" he asked with a slightly icy glare.

She turned to him then looked back at Paul. Paul smiled at her knowing who she truly wanted to be with. He leaned in a gave her a quick kiss on the cheek, "magic is in the air, have a good night." He jigged his way off the dance floor.

The next song was much slower. Jason brushed his fingers through Molly's hair before wrapping his arms around her pulling her close up against him. She wished she could stay strong and keep her feelings in check but she was melting into him. She laid her head against his chest as they swayed back and forth to the slow rhythm of the music.

When the song was over Jason grabbed her hand, "let's go for a walk." She did not protest as he led her off the floor. They followed the walkway over to the beach. Molly kicked off her sandals and dug her toes into the cool sand.

Molly could feel Jason's tension coming back. She did not want the entire trip to be like this. They had to sort this out, she turned to face him but he spoke first.

"Were you trying to make me jealous?" he asked with a slight edge to his voice.

She could not help but laugh a little. "Not at first. I really was just trying to have fun. Your conversation with Anna was a reality check for me so I found someone else to hang out with. But I can't help my feelings when I see you," she softened her voice partly because she was nervous. "So maybe I was trying to make you jealous. But it wasn't right of me to do that." She smiled up at him, "it figures that the first guy in six years that I like is practically engaged."

Jason was not smiling back, he was peering into her soul again, intensifying her desire for him. She could not take her eyes off him. He stepped closer and held her head in his hands. She closed her eyes. His lips were gently brushing her eyelids. Her breathing quickened as he traced down to her lips. One hand moved to the back of her head while the other started gently gliding down her bare back. His lips finally found hers setting her whole body on fire. His first touch was soft but then his tongue demanded more. She parted her lips to let him in to taste. Their kiss deepened and Molly gripped onto his back pushing her hips into him feeling his need for her grow. She was excited and scared at the same time. She stepped back from his embrace out of breath.

"So what do we do now?" she asked him.

He held his hand on her cheek and smiled. "I know what I'm doing, turning off all the phones." He leaned in to kiss her again but she stepped back.

"Jason, it's been a long time for me."

He pulled her into an embrace. "It's okay, you pick the pace, no pressure, let's just have fun together." He leaned in for another kiss, he would settle for the sweet taste of her lips.

Chapter 11

Back in the room they took turns getting ready to settle in for the evening. Katie had snuck a revealing nightie into Molly's suitcase but she did not want to lead Jason on so she opted for a tank top and shorts. When she came out of the bathroom she found Jason laying back on the bed wearing just a pair of shorts. She wished he would put a shirt on, she wanted to run her hands over his bare chest which would likely lead her to a place she was not yet ready for. She needed a distraction so she grabbed all the brochures she picked up early that day and headed over to the bed. She sat down on the edge keeping a slight distance between the two of them. "Shall we pick out some things to do?"

He could think of a few things to do with her right this second. How come she could not be wearing flannel pajamas? The swell of her breasts under her tank was driving him crazy. Everything she wore drove him crazy. Even though he was hot he slid under the blankets to hide his desire for her. He saw the brochures spread out on the bed when he realized she asked him a question. He did not care much what they did. He wanted her to pick, it was her trip, "whatever you want to do is fine."

"It's your trip too, pick something," she said as she was sorting out the brochures.

He started to look through them just to amuse her. He vacationed mostly in cities or on the ski slopes and he knew she had never been anywhere. He had no idea what would suit them both.

"This is what I want to do," Molly bounced up. "Zip lining, look eleven lines across the tree canopy. I really want to do this, can we?"

"Absolutely," anything to make her happy.

"Okay you pick next."

He sifted through the brochures trying to think what she would like. He found a tour that would take all day but it sounded fun. "How about his one, boat ride around the island, hike into the mountains to a waterfall, lunch then snorkeling."

"I'm not sure about the snorkeling but the rest sounds good." He felt better, he seemed to make a good choice, he hoped she would pick the rest.

"This local craft market sounds nice too, oh and don't forget you need some new clothes," she added chuckling. She set aside the brochures of choice. "Oh look there's a big street party every Friday night."

"I like the sound of that especially if you dress up again."

Molly was looking through the rest of the brochures when she remembered something from earlier on in the day, "by the way what did Katie say to you at the airport?"

He pushed all the brochures off the bed and pulled Molly up against him. "She said you wanted me naked." Molly's whole body tensed, she looked him in the eye and noticed his evil grin. She was not sure if he was kidding but she decided to let it go. Half of her wanted to push away from the him but she also wanted his warmth and security so she wrapped her leg across him and put her head on his chest. He rubbed her back until she drifted off into a peaceful sleep.

Jason had spent a good portion of the night watching Molly sleep. She was so peaceful and she fit perfectly into his side. He could hold her and feel like he was protecting her from the world.

He did fall asleep eventually but when he woke up he was alone. He looked at the bed and it was a mess. He must have been tossing and turning. He remembered seeing flashes of both Anna and Molly in his dreams. He could not remember any specifics about the dreams but it was obviously a reflection of what was going on in his life. He turned over and realized he was alone. He sat up to see Molly sitting outside, he pushed the images out of his mind.

He went outside and joined her at the table. She had already gotten breakfast. There were plates of fruit and pastries as well as a carafe of coffee.

"Good morning." She smiled up at him. "Sleep well?"

He rubbed his hand through his hair, "not really."

"Oh, sorry. I think I slept better than I have in a long time." She wondered why he had a rough night. She was also hoping for a better greeting than that, maybe something that involved a kiss. She hoped he was not going to change his mind about her. She wanted to cheer him up. "I brought us some breakfast. I did not get anything hot. I was not sure how long you were going to be asleep. The coffee is still hot though." She poured him a cup and slid it across the table.

"Thank you," he said but with not much emotion. "Do you always get up early when you are on vacation?"

Wow he was crabby in the morning. "I don't know I've never been on vacation, remember?"

He sighed and closed his eyes. "I'm sorry."

"I know we are facing west but it was really amazing to see the light coming up changing the color of the sky and water. It was like the sun was giving the earth a giant hug good morning. There was a band of pink wrapping around the horizon as if to say it's going to be a beautiful day." She thought of how the water started to sparkle and the pelicans started flying low and diving for their early morning breakfast. She turned to look at Jason as he stared blankly at the ocean. "Besides I can only sleep when there are busses and taxis honking out my window." She laughed hoping to get a response from him.

He did smile but stayed silent. She watched him munching on a croissant. He still looked deep in thought but did not want to guess what he thinking. She noticed that he left the Tiffany's box on the dresser. It would be a good reminder for her that this was just a fantasy. But while she was here and living it she was going to enjoy it. She had to do something to snap him out of his mood. "Red or black?" she asked him.

"What?" he asked looking at her quizzically.

"Red or black?" she repeated.

"I don't know either sounds good."

"It's not a difficult question, choose one," she insisted. She knew he never made decisions. She did get him to choose an activity last night so she wanted to keep him thinking.

Simple decision, right, sure he thought to himself, there was never a simple answer to anything when it came to women. Whatever he chose she would likely pick the opposite. That was what Anna always did anyway. She never really wanted his opinion, just pretended she cared. Molly did seem to care though. What was she referring to anyway he wondered. She probably would not tell him.

"Hello Jason, the beach is waiting."

"Black then," he blurted out still having no idea what he was choosing. He continued sitting while she went inside. He let his mind go blank as he watched the water, the sailboats and the birds flying by. Molly was right. It was easy to do soul searching with a view like this except he was afraid he would find his soul empty so he sat staring at the sea sipping his coffee.

He still had not been able to completely relax himself when the patio door opened. It was a good thing he had not been holding his coffee cup because he would have dropped it. Molly was standing there in a black string bikini. It showed off her flat stomach, slight curves and beautiful breasts. Black, good choice but he couldn't wait to see red.

Molly watched him as he looked her over slowly from toes to chest and finally to her eyes. She was learning to enjoy the attention from him. She held out a bottle of sunscreen, "can you help me with this?" Her voice was a little raspy with nervousness.

He watched as her chest rose with her cute nervous breaths. Hell yeah he could help her and do a lot more too but he remembered he had to let her pick the pace. And if she said no it was going to be a rough day at the beach staring at her all day.

He took the bottle from her and followed her back into the room. The view from the back was equally as hot. The beads at the end of her strings were swaying with her walk. He was getting hotter by the second. He lightly touched her shoulders to stop her but kept her facing away from him. He poured sunscreen on his hands and started rubbing it into the smooth skin of her shoulders.

She shuddered at his touch but it was from pleasure. She was so heated from the way he looked at her she did not even notice the coolness of the lotion on her skin. She relaxed back into his hands enjoying every second of his gentle touch. She could tell he wasn't just getting the sunscreen on but exploring her back not missing a spot. She felt her top go loose and she almost instinctively covered up but strong hands held her arms in place.

"I don't want to miss a spot or leave funky lines," he whispered in her ear.

She could not stand the heat anymore, she needed him more than she thought she needed anything. She turned to face him and put her hands on his still bare chest. She reached up to meet his lips and kissed him deeply, hungrily. She moved her hands into the mess of his hair and pulled her hips firmly against his. She could feel his throbbing desire for her. She was ready and slowly moved against him to let him know.

He was out of breath and almost in pain with his need for her. "Please say no now. If we keep going I'm not going to be able to stop this time." He kissed her cheeks and started moving down her neck waiting for her to reply.

"I want you Jason." She tipped her head back taking in the pleasure of his lips.

It was his signal to go lower. His lips travelled down to the swell of her breasts. He took one in each hand gently rubbing the outer edges of her nipples. He felt her stagger a little so picked her up and gently laid her down on the bed. He slid her top off followed by her bottoms. He resumed his tender love making on her breasts letting his tongue do the dancing this time. He slid one hand down her side feeling her muscles tense. He ran his hand along the outer edges of her thigh before coming back up on the inside.

Molly was swimming with pleasure. She was trying to take in all the spots that made her tingle but every place he touched sent a new wave of electricity through her body. When his fingers reached inside her she whimpered from a sensation she never knew existed. As his finger gently explored her it pushed her pleasure to new heights. His lips came back up to meet hers. She wrapped her arms around his back digging in, holding on to something solid to let her know this was real. She pushed her hips up wanting more and he gave her more until she tightened around him feeling her whole body shudder than collapse. She held onto him not wanting to let go, not wanting this moment to pass.

He did a quick shimmy away form her, his pain was increasing. He reached into the nightstand and quickly slid on a condom. He knew she had not had sex in a long time and she was tight. He climbed on top of her and gently, slowly slid inside of her. He watched her face as he held still for a moment, he did not want to cause her any pain. When she wrapped her legs around him he knew she was okay. He brushed her sweaty hair off her face kissing the moisture from her eyes, nose and then her lips. He moved slowly inside of her until he could not resist any longer. He could feel her legs tightening around him as he started going deeper and harder. Her hips came up off the bed and he exploded with all the pent up feelings he has had for her the last few weeks. He groaned with the release and rolled over on his back pulling her on top of him. Now he refused to let her go but she managed to slide off him.

She licked the salty sweat of his lips before plunging in for another passionate kiss. She could feel him start to swell again so she pulled back and sat up. She looked into his eyes holding his gaze, savoring his desire for her. She broke into a smile. "That was amazing, but," she said slowly, "I do want to make it out of this room today."

He pulled her back onto him. "Why? I have no problem staying in."

She rolled off him throwing a pillow at his head. "Well I have an island to see." She sauntered off into the bathroom.

And I got my view he thought as he watched her sway across the room. He rolled back onto the bed and drifted off into a peaceful sleep this time.

He could wake up every day this way. Molly was leaning over him brushing her lips across his eyes. She smiled when he opened them. He smiled back at her looking lovely in a flowing but short sundress. He sat up "I thought you wanted to go to the beach today."

"I thought we could do a little shopping instead." She saw him wince and remembered his complaints of always having to shop with Anna. "You need new clothes remember?"

"I don't need any clothes if we stay here," he raised his eyebrows at her.

She backed away before he could pull her down again. "I want to go to the local craft market also. Come on it will be fun."

"Okay," he rolled out of bed.

They took the resort shuttle to the local market. They strolled in and out of the vendor spaces. Molly could not believe how may different things one could make with coconuts and palm leaves. They had a laugh when she put on a coconut bra and straw hat. She wondered off by herself. She wanted to pick out something for Jason. What do you get for someone who probably has everything? She decided on a pen set made from local hardwoods. This way he would think of her while he was working. She wandered around some more and picked out one more thing for him.

They moved on to an upscale shopping center where the cruise ships dock. She sent Jason off to pick out some new clothes while she milled around more souvenir shops. He was glad since he really wanted to pick out something special for her. At some points they met up and then separated again. He never experienced this kind of shopping before. He was able to spend a little more time looking for things he wanted or what he thought Molly would like.

When they were back on the bus she showed him some of the picture frames and wall hangings she bought to dress up the walls of her apartment. He showed her the clothes he picked. She liked the variety of casual to island dressy.

Back at the hotel they decided to eat at the dressier table service restaurant. She changed into a longer dress and only because it was required he changed into a collared shirt and long pants. They eyed each other as they both left the room each holding a package from the days shopping.

They timed the reservation so they could watch the sunset first. They sat on a chair on the beach. Jason was behind her. She leaned into his embrace as she watched the sun slowly dip towards the horizon. She took pictures every few minutes as the glow of the water turned from pinks to fiery orange. They watched in complete contented silence. The sun gave one last wink as it dipped to awaken a far away land. The night sky was suddenly dark.

Molly turned to Jason not worried about him seeing the water filling her eyes. "Every time I think I could never see anything more beautiful something else comes along."

He knew what she meant but was afraid to say it. Every day, every moment he saw her he discovered a new beauty in her. And he was seeing the beauty she saw in everything around them no matter where they were. He leaned forward and kissed the single tear running down her cheek.

After they were seated in the restaurant with drinks on the table Molly pulled out her bag. "Do you want to see what I got you?"

"You didn't have to get me anything."

"I know, I wanted to though." She pulled out a rectangular box and handed it over to him. "This is for your desk."

He opened the box to find two pens made from beautiful red and dark brown woods, he ran his hand over the smooth surface. It also came with a stand but the wood was rough and kept in a more natural shape. "This is really nice."

"Do you like it? I know it's not the most unique gift but I thought it would be a nicer souvenir than some of the other things we saw. And it's useful too."

He laughed a little as she went on, "relax I really do like my gift."

"Well I have something else for you." She handed over a bag.

He pulled out a a black woven Baja styled pull over. It was long sleeve with a hood. The inside was brushed over to feel like fleece. He slipped it over his head. "I have always wanted one of these."

"Liar!"

"No really, I just, well I don't know."

"Well it looks nice on you." She cleared her throat before she added. "I have to admit that I also bought it because I know Anna would hate it. Was that wrong of me?" She gave him a wicked grin.

"Yes," but he did not care, he leaned over and kissed her softly. "I bought something for you also." He also had a rectangular box that he handed over to her.

She held the box for a moment. She slowly opened the lid to find a silver necklace. Hanging from the center were two flying doves attached to each other. They were outlined in silver and gold and were encrusted in small diamonds.

"It reminds me of you and Julie and the freedom you had together."

Molly did not know what to say. No one had ever given her anything so thoughtful in her life. This actually meant more to her than this trip. "It's beautiful," she said softly still staring at the two birds. Her hands shook as she picked it up out of the box.

Jason got up and took the necklace from her. He clasped it around her neck then knelt down by her side. She was still holding the doves in her hand when she finally turned to look at him.

"Like I said every time I think I have seen the most beautiful thing something with even more beauty comes along." She leaned down to kiss him.

His heart melted at her words and the softness of her lips. He was frozen in his spot, unable to move or respond. Luckily the waiter came by with their dinner plates. He caressed her cheek then got up and returned to his seat.

After dinner Molly led Jason back out onto the beach to watch the night sky. They found an empty beach chair. Jason sat first and Molly leaned back on him pulling his arms around her. She could have spent the whole night with him on that chair. She was so relaxed she almost did doze off when she jumped up and pointed out a shooting star to Jason.

"Make a wish," Jason said.

"How about we make one wish we keep to ourselves and one wish we tell each other."

"You first," since he could not think of what to say. He wished he could stay here with Molly. He did not want to face the end of the week where there would be decisions to be made. He was carefree and relaxed and he knew Molly played a big part in that.

"I want to be able to pay for someone's college education. I can create some obscure scholarship that would help a young women defeat hard times and achieve her goals."

"Kind of like yourself."

"Yes, a payback for the help I got for school. Your turn."

How do you beat that, he wondered. So he said the only logical thing. "I wish for your wish to come true."

Molly gave him a crooked smile. "That's cheating."

"Why? You did not ask for anything for yourself. So now your wish is doubled and will surely come true."

"Well thanks." It was a nice gesture but she knew he, once again, was avoiding making any kind of choices for himself. Maybe he did have everything or at least access to whatever he wanted. She wondered what that would be like when he interrupted her thoughts.

"There must be something you would want for yourself after all these years." Maybe he could help her out.

She was such a practical person that she did not know how to answer. "Other than travel, I'm not really sure. I learned early in life that if there is something you want you have to work hard and go after it. Right now I have everything I need."

"But need is different than a wish or something that you don't think about because it's out of your reach."

She had not thought much beyond the next year. What would she like someday? "How about something bigger than a studio apartment? That would be a big wish on a teachers salary in the city."

"But the fact that you even have your place means that your wish is achievable. What else?" He wanted to know her every wish and desire.

But she was done, she did not want her true wish to slip. "That's it, one for you and one for me to keep." She smiled and gave him a soft lingering kiss. When she pulled away she taunted him by saying, "I need to shower."

Jason immediately scooped her up in his arms and carried her all the way back to their room. On the way she kissed his neck and his chin. He walked faster as his body burned with desire. He managed to hold onto her as he pulled out the room key and unlocked the door. He finally set her down when they were in the bathroom, he barely let go to turn on the water.

Molly pulled his shirt off and continued her kissing down his throat across his chest. She gave each of his nipples extra attention. She was rewarded with a deep throated groan from Jason. He was barely able to stand as she made her way down to his navel and skimmed across the top edge of his shorts. In a quick motion she had his pants down to the ground but before she took him to the point of no return he lifted her up to him. Kissing her hard and deep he unzipped her dress and let it fall to the ground. He just as quickly disposed of her undies and backed her into the shower.

Molly made a quick grab for the soap and started making her way across his broad shoulders and down his center. She added a light touch with her fingernails. He tucked his arms under hers and melted his weight against her. She continued circling down his back and across his firm buttocks. She brought both hands around to his front and lightly caressed his erection with the soap.

Jason's mind went hazy. He pushed them back against the wall to steady himself. Her caresses were bringing him close to explosion but he wanted them to climax together this time.

Molly obliged when when he raised her arms. She switched to massaging his scalp but wanting to continue arousing him. She wrapped one leg around him and pressed her hips into him. He pulled her even closer with one hand on her buttock, the other massaging her breast. She kissed him deeply while slowing rocking her hips against him making him harder.

Jason was losing control, he was breathing hard, he needed to take her now and hoped he could bring them to ecstasy together. He stepped out for one quick moment and came back ready. He lifted her up and she wrapped both her legs around him. He entered her soft warmth and held them both still to savor the rush of electricity jolting through their bodies. He sat them on the edge of the built in bench and pulled her body close to him. She whimpered in his ear which created another pulse of excitement.

Molly squeezed her legs even tighter around him. She wanted to feel all of him. She massaged his head, rubbed his back, kissed his neck and his ear. With every new thing she did he let out a little moan. She finally pressed her lips hard against his as she rocked deeper and harder onto him. They needed to breath so they held onto their embrace as the rocked together until the last hard thrust that brought them both to climax. They collapsed onto each other exhausted but completely satisfied emotionally and physically.

She did not want to let go, she probably could not even if the fire alarm went off. She closed her eyes and let every last bit of tension melt out of her muscles. Jason held on to her as he gently washed her hair and her body. When he was done he wrapped a towel around her and carried her to the bed. He laid her on her side and wrapped himself around her. Their body rhythms were completed in sync. They both felt loved, maybe even in love but neither one was going to say it so they just held on to each other, holding onto the moment before drifting off into a blissful sleep.

The next few days were a chain of adrenaline rushes. The zip lining was the most frightening but amazing thing Molly had ever done. Just like her doves she felt free flying from one tree top to the next. Jason was thrilled to be out in the natural world. He cheered Molly on as the zip lines got longer and higher. He rewarded her with hugs and kisses at the end of each line.

The next day they spent the entire day lounging on the beach. Of course it took them a while to get there as the red bikini did not stay on Molly any longer then the black one did. When they did get out they strolled the sandy beaches and climbed around the rocks, Molly experimented with her camera. Jason took some shots of her pretending she was a swimsuit model.

They spent the evenings watching the nightly line up of entertainers. They met up with Paul and some of the other couples. They were able to talk freely with no judgements over who had what. They watched the sunset and waited for shooting stars before making love to cap off their days.

They went on the day long tour that Jason had picked out for them. The small yacht took them out into the ocean following the coastline. Molly continued playing budding photographer capturing the changing scenery. Jason stood behind her holding her steady with his embrace as the boat skimmed across the gentle waves. The Pitons, the twin mountains that were the icons of St. Lucia came into view. They were covered in lush greenery which changed colors with the passing clouds casting shadows on them.

The boat docked at a local fishing village where they were taken into the mountains to hike to a waterfall. Molly of course had never seen one in person before and was amazed at the continuous flow of water. She was memorized by the water splashing, bouncing and reflecting all the colors of the rainbow. She reluctantly left as the tour was heading to lunch in the village. She did become grateful though as in true tropical rainforest style it did start to rain as they neared the end of the trail.

After the lunch the boat headed over to a local snorkeling spot. Molly was not a confident swimmer but Jason convinced her to put on a life vest and join him. The water was deep and cold but refreshing. He showed her how to use the face mask and snorkel. He held her hand as they let the current take them closer to the shore where they could see more fish. Molly focused on slow regular breathing while letting the life vest carry her weight. She held onto Jason tightly, there was no way she would let herself drift off alone.

The water cleared and they were able to see a variety of fish of different sizes and colors. Molly hoped there would be no sharks. While it was amazing to be in the ocean with all its life it was still a little out of her comfort zone so she pointed back to the boat. Jason helped her swim back and they climbed back on board

"You are incredibly brave," he smiled and helped her out of her vest.

"I don't feel it," she shivered from the cool water.

"Well I'm glad you came with me."

"Thanks for taking me, I'm glad I did it."

"Mind if I swim around some more."

"No, go ahead."

Molly wrapped herself in a towel and watched as he swam to a new spot. She was amazed when he dove under the water with the snorkel and laughed when he came back up and blew water out of it. If that had been her she probably would have choked and drowned. She took more photos of him wanting to catch him in his state of freedom. Eventually he made his way back as it was time to head back to the marina.

They sat back on a lounger letting the sun dry and warm them back up.

"That was a lot of fun," Jason commented to her.

"I'm glad you picked this tour, I really enjoyed it and I got to do a whole lot of things I never have all in one day."

Jason was glad to hear that. Not only did he get to do some of his favorite activities he got do to them with Molly. She was brave, adventurous and thoughtful of him. "What has been your favorite activity so far?"

She smiled at him seductively and leaned closer to him. "You." She brushed his lips with hers tasting the salt water. She kissed all around his mouth before pressing his lips apart. She kissed him hard and passionately. She wanted him to feel and understand what he meant to her and she wanted him to remember it long past this moment.

When they pulled apart Jason nestled her against him. He closed his eyes taking in her scent and feel committing it to his memory. Hs could feel his heart aligning with hers. He remembered the lady who told them their auras were blending. He was not sure where he should go from here. He came here expecting one thing but now his plans and the whole course of his life could be shifting. He thought he had found love but with Molly the idea of love was decidedly different and he had no idea what to do about it.

Molly tuned over and held his head in her hands. "In case I forgot to tell you, thank you for bringing me here. Thank you for sharing this adventure with me and thank you for sharing yourself."

Love, he thought, yes he could love her, already did love her. But that was the easy part. Give her what she wanted? He was not sure he could do that. Maybe though, maybe by the end of the week he could face that decision.

The boat docked and she rolled off him. "Let's stay in and get room service tonight."

"I like the sound of that," he whispered in her ear kissing her neck giving her a preview of what was to come.

They got back to the room tired but elated. Jason entered the room and was bombarded by a tall blond squealing at him.

"Yes, yes, and yes." Anna threw herself on Jason.

Chapter 12

It took a few seconds for Molly to realize what was happening. She watched in stunned silence as Anna pulled Jason deeper into the room. He seemed just as shocked as she was.

When he was finally able to speak he asked her what she was talking about.

"The ring Jason, I couldn't help myself when I saw the box, of course I will marry you." She held the ring in front of her just as Molly had done only a few days ago. "It's perfect."

"I can't believe you are here." Jason was still shocked he did not know what else to say.

"Well I figured a few days couldn't hurt. Now I know why you wanted me to come so desperately.

By the way I changed our flights so we can fly to Italy straight from here."

Anna peered back to Molly. "Don't worry sweetie I kept your flight the same."

Molly's world was tilting, the room was spinning, she needed to get away. The only place she could go was the bathroom. She splashed cold water on her face. She needed to get herself under control at least until she could get out of the room. The room, that was a problem, someone had to go. There was no way she was staying here. Maybe she should just fly home. It was only two more days, she wanted to stay, it was still her vacation even if it meant seeing Jason and Anna together. She took a few deep breaths and gathered her toiletries together.

She stepped out of the room and politely interrupted Anna. She was already talking about wedding plans. "Excuse me Jason?"

He did hear her since he turned to look at her but he was still dazed.

"Jason," she said a little more loudly to make sure he was listening. "This might get a little awkward. Maybe we can see if there is another room available I can move to?"

He was definitely processing information slower but he caught on. "Oh, right, let me call the front desk."

"Actually if you give me a few minutes I can pack quickly and I will walk down with you." Her plan was that if there was no room available she would head to the airport and fly home right away and she did not want to come back to get her luggage.

"Yeah sure that's fine."

Molly was glad they had kept the room fairly neat. It made the packing easier and quicker and there was no outright evidence of their love making. She was thankful for that for both her and Jason. When she was done she turned to Anna and in her most cheerful voice she could muster she said, "congratulations, you are a lucky woman." Anna did not respond as she was admiring her ring so she turned to Jason, "I'm ready."

She followed Jason out the door. He held his head low and his hands were stuffed in his pockets. After a few steps he took her suitcase from her but they walked to the front desk in silence. Jason made arrangements for her to stay in another oceanfront room but it was on the other side of the main pool and restaurant area. That was good Molly thought, they would be less likely to run into each other just walking around.

They followed the signs to her new room and Jason let her in. It was pretty much the same as the other room. King bed, beautiful views of the ocean. She was starting to lose her cool. She would not be able to look at Jason any more. She walked over to the french doors and opened them up to let the breeze in. "Thanks, you can go now," she told him as a tear started falling down her cheek.

He hesitated but decided to go to her. "I'm sorry," he said as he ran his fingers through her hair.

She gathered the courage to face him, "it's not your fault. We both knew this was how it was going to end. Maybe a small part of me hoped it wouldn't but . . . anyway it just happened a few days earlier than we planned."

He rubbed the tears off her cheeks and tried to pull her closer. "I don't know what to say."

And that was the problem she thought as she pulled away from him. "There is nothing to say, the Jason I want to be with," her heart was beating fast but she had to say it, "the one I love, is the person you are with me. You are different around Anna, and I don't like that Jason as much. So you can go, we'll both go back to our lives. I will always cherish this experience but I need you to leave now."

He knew she was closing herself up again, going back into her self protective mode. He didn't think he would be able to stop it. Everything was happening too fast and he was not ready to face this. He was confused about his feelings for both of them and now she was accusing him of being two people. He didn't want to leave angry but he couldn't stay. He dropped her room key on the bed and walked out, walked back to the life he had always known.

Molly was a little reluctant to get up the next morning but she knew she only had a few mornings left to see the new days light dance on the water. When she stepped out on the patio there was a covered plate, a drink carafe, flowers and a note on the table. She opened the card. I will also always cherish our time together. That was it? That was all he could think of to say? Despite her irritation she was not going to let the food go to waste. At least he remembered what her favorites were, fruits and sweet pastries. That actually added to her irritation since that was one of the things that she liked about him, the way that he paid so much attention to her.

She finished her breakfast, showered and put on her hot red bikini. It was somewhat deliberate. She did want to look good for herself and as a reminder of what he was missing, that was if Anna did not keep him locked up in the room. Well whatever happened she was going to try to enjoy the day.

Molly found a spot on the beach with two lounge chairs and an umbrella. She settled in and read her book for a while. She never had time to read at home so she brought a few books with her but so far Jason had kept her sufficiently occupied. After getting through a few chapters she saw Paul walk by and motioned for him to join her.

He sat down next to her, "by yourself today?" he asked surprised.

Lesley Esposito

"The girlfriend, excuse me fiancé flew in last night to surprise him. She found the ring, put it on and now they are engaged," she added with a sneer.

"Wow," he replied knowing there was really nothing else he could say to make her feel better.

"So will you keep me company?"

"Absolutely."

She had him apply sunscreen to her back. It was definitely not the same sultry feeling she got when Jason lathered her up. It was a confirmation in a way of her desire, of her to need to feel Jason, but she couldn't have him.

"You know you look extremely sexy in this bikini?" Paul whispered in her ear while rubbing lotion on her shoulders.

"I have heard that," she replied with a blushed smile. It was still nice to hear a compliment from any man.

"Are you expecting a certain person to see you on the beach?"

"It was for you Paul," she smiled at him teasingly.

"I wish, but I know better and good for you, make him jealous."

"If the witch even lets him out, besides Anna is so beautiful anyway he probably won't notice me anymore."

"Darling, there is not a man here that has not noticed you."

"Thanks Paul," she said giving him a hug.

They spent the morning and early afternoon lounging, swimming and taking photographs. Paul was quite proficient with the camera and showed Molly how to use the manual settings. She took closeups and long exposure shots, he made her see things in different ways. She was looking forward to taking some fabulous sunset shots. She was even thinking about the city and how she could see things differently through her camera.

After lunch they were back on the lounge chairs when Molly saw Anna and Jason making their way on to the beach. As usual Anna looked fantastic in a gold two piece bikini with a flowing sarong and large sunglasses. The outfit was probably more than her house payment Molly thought to herself. Maybe even three or four especially when you added in the sandals that wrapped up her toned calves. Jason was following her carrying the towels, tote bag, water bottles. He was already sweating but he was also wearing linen pants and a button up shirt. Molly did not remember seeing those clothes before. She wondered why he was not wearing his bathing suit. Anna actually did not look too comfortable either. You could tell she was pouting about the heat as she looked around for shade. Luckily for her there was still an umbrella left and luckily for Molly it was on the other side of the beach. If Paul was right when he said all the men noticed her, she was definitely being replaced by Anna. Even Paul was looking.

"I told you she was beautiful."

"Sure if you like that high class spend all my money kind of look. Actually everyone is looking because she does not look like she belongs here. She looks like she belongs on a private island getting a private massage. Everyone is probably just figuring out who she is."

"Thanks for trying to make me feel better" she smiled at him, "but there is no denying she is gorgeous. Should I go over and say hi?"

"Not a chance, besides I will bet he will be over here shortly."

"I guess we will find out."

Molly could not sit still after a while and decided to go for a swim. She was starting to relax letting the water ripple over her while she floated on her back. She was lost in her thoughts when she suddenly felt something brush under her back. She jumped from the tingling sensation and tried to find the source. When she stood up she opened her eyes to see Jason standing in front of her. He was looking at her with such longing that she was uncomfortable. She tried to swim away but he grabbed her arm and pulled her back.

"Leave me alone," she said softly as she tried to leave again.

"We don't have to ignore each other," he said still holding on to her. "Besides it would look weird."

"Look weird?" she asked confused, then she understood. "Oh you mean to Anna, maybe she would think we were hiding something?"

He stood there jaw clamped. She was not making this easy. "Maybe."

"Well I would not worry. Anna could care less about me, if she thought I was a threat I would not be here. But then again maybe if she found out it would make your life easier, one less decision to make. Isn't that what you always want, someone else to decide for you?"

She was infuriating him but he needed to set the tone for the last two days. "Please?" he asked, "can we just be cordial to each other?"

She pulled put of his grip but did not move, "fine, let's see, how are you? Weather looks good today, water a little chilly, oh, I did not know you were wearing a bathing suit," Molly said to him matter of fact.

"Oh, you mean the linens, Anna would only come out on the beach if I agreed to take some photos with her, I think she plans on using them for the engagement announcements."

Molly was now completely deflated and irritated. Jason was still with Anna yet still toying with her. She starting heading back to the beach.

"Jason, just go back to Anna and leave me alone!" Molly said thinking she could not move through the water fast enough.

"Molly wait, what did I say?" he managed to grab her elbow and spin her back around to face him again.

"Really? You think I want to hear about all this wedding crap. You know how I feel about you."

He did and he still had feelings for her. He stepped up to her and said in a low voice "maybe I can come up to your room tonight."

Bastard, she could not believe her ears. "Hell no you can't do that don't even think about it. You are engaged and she is here."

"But it was okay while she was not here?" he challenged her.

"You know what you are right, it was not okay", Molly calmed down a bit. She hesitated and looked deeply into his eyes and added "but I did not regret one second of it, I just can't keep it up Jason."

Jason let go of her and watched as she walked out of the water. She packed up her things, said something to Paul and walked off. He was extremely jealous of Paul but he knew nothing happened between them, not the way he responded to her. She was right, he should not have teased her that way but he had no control when he was around her. Then when he went back to Anna he no control over anything. She just took over and told him what to do, what to wear, how to live. It was easy, she made his life easy and he liked it that way, didn't he? This was where his life was supposed to go. A good degree, a good job following his fathers footsteps, a great woman your family liked and approved of then you get married. There was nothing wrong with that. So what do you do when one woman, a hot sexy woman you randomly meet throws a monkey wrench in you life? Is that what following your heart was and if so what should he do about everything else? He looked over to Anna decided there was no do over for him.

Jason made a reservation at the wait service restaurant since he knew Anna would not go anywhere near the buffet. He also wanted to have a quiet dinner just for the two of them. They were sharing a bottle of wine discussing wedding locations. Well Anna was discussing he was agreeing, ultimately he would make very few if any decisions about the wedding, but he knew for sure that was typical for the groom-to-be.

He was mostly staying focused until Molly and Paul walked in. Damn her, why was she torturing him with his favorite long dress that was cut low down the back. She had her arm wrapped around Paul smiling and laughing with him. They stopped at their table.

"Jason, Anna, hope you are enjoying your dinner. Jason thank you again for the camera, Paul has been showing me how to take some great sunset photos." Molly smiled at them as they continued on to their table.

"Don't they make a cute couple," Anna smiled at them and continued listing possible wedding sites.

Hell no, Jason thought to himself but he would keep that to himself. "I think we would need to figure out how many guests then we can narrow the possibilities down" he said trying to focus back on the conversation. Anna just gave him a little smile and squeezed his hand. Of course she knew that, oh well he let her carry on talking about guests, the wedding party, food and whatever else. Jason was listening but mostly because Molly and Paul were sitting too far away to hear what they were saying. He did not like the easy laughter they were sharing and he did not like that she never once looked to catch a glimpse of him.

It was killing Molly not to look over at Jason. She knew Anna was going on about the wedding. She heard her on the way in and she was glad she could not hear her now. She knew Anna was glowing and she had every right to be, she was going to be a stunning bride. Paul was keeping her occupied, carrying most of the conversation, telling funny stories from his football games and teaching. He insisted that she not look back at the couple and he was right. She had to start getting over him. He was not the first person she had to get over. One more day and back to her life. Finish school and move on and ignore the social pages in the newspaper. She wondered if it would be a spring or fall wedding. Too hot in the summer, that she knew. Big and elaborate most likely with hundreds of guests. Definitely not her style. She never thought about what her own wedding would be like. Small for sure, maybe on a beach at sunrise, not sunset. Sunrise was the dawn of a new day, full of hope just like start of a new marriage.

Later that evening there was a knock on the door. She figured it might be Paul so she opened the door without checking. It was Jason. He walked in without being invited. She really did not want him here but followed him in anyway.

"I just wanted to check on you," he said pushing her hair away from her eyes.

She stepped away. She could not take his touch anymore it was causing too much pain, she needed to start distancing herself from him. "Jason, I knew my heart was going to be broken at the end of this week. I told myself it did not matter but there was a little piece of me that could dream." She looked away. That was as close as she would come to asking him to stay.

Molly sat on the bed as she watched Jason pacing back and forth. The air was getting thick with tension but she knew this might be one of her last chances to talk to him, she had to say what was on her mind. "Someone once told me that maybe it was not me that needed saving. Maybe this trip was more about you and not me and that is why we were brought together. Maybe our meeting was not as random as we thought."

He turned, eyebrows punched together, "what the hell does that mean, what do I need saving from, there is nothing wrong with my life."

"Sure if you like being told what to do all the time." She could see his anger rising, she did not want to anger him just open his eyes. "I'm going to miss you but not the Jason that is with Anna, I'm going to miss the Jason that is with me. The one that is free, adventurous, kind and caring and has an opinion."

What the hell, he was all those things, he was still angry. "And what about you, you don't need saving from your dull social life?"

That stung. He knew her situation. Now she was angry. "Well maybe I will use some of the new social skills you taught me when I get home," she spat back at him.

He punched the wall, he did not want her with other men. And she did not want him with Anna. His hands started to tremble, he needed to leave, be by himself so headed for the door.

"Good night Jason, have a nice life," she yelled after him.

She was still angry when she went to bed but she was sad also. She did not intend to end things that way. She was also mad at herself for letting herself fall so hard for him. She would have to get over it but the memories of their few days together were so strong and fresh. She fell asleep dreaming of a wedding. She could see the light yellows and pink of the sky with a cool morning breeze letting her veil trail softly behind her. The groom was a blur but she was at peace and elated all at once. There were only a few guests sprinkled on the sand but it was everyone she cared about. As dreams do it skipped to the kiss and she felt the physical desire in her sleep. The heat and lust made her think of Jason then she woke breathing hard feeling the need to hold him again. She sighed, sad for the dream to end and sad knowing she would not get what she wanted or needed from Jason. She wondered if you truly could find that feeling again in someone else or do you really find love only once. And was that love she found with Jason, she had no way of knowing. Do you stop with the first person you think you love? Well she would keep looking, she had no choice, eventually after school.

She got up to see the beautiful morning unfold once again. When she went out to the patio not only was breakfast there so was the person who delivered it. Jason looked restless yet he was unmoving just staring out to the ocean. There were storm clouds out in the distance giving the sky an eerie gray mixed in with the yellow and pink hues. He had a firm grip on his coffee mug but he was not drinking. Molly sat down quietly next to him knowing it was his mind that was restless, there was not much left to say to him so she left him alone to his thoughts.

He was thinking that Molly knew exactly what he needed which was the quiet of the early morning. He already had enough talk of the wedding. As hard as he tried he just could not picture the day. It should be happy and joyous and yet he was anxious. Here was peace and comfort. Yet things were set in motion and he had no idea how to stop it and still was undecided if he should. Italy was up next, Molly would be at home and maybe that would put things in perspective. Was it really possible to fall in love with another person and out of love with the one you are with so easily? Well it was not making his life easy anyway and that is what he was used to, easy. What would be easy was having Molly yell and scream at him instead of the peace she gave him. It actually irritated him at the moment that she was so damned understanding. Now he could not stand the silence anymore, apparently she could not either.

"Do you always get up this early on your day off?" She asked with a smile hoping to ease the tension between them.

He smiled back at her remembering the way he asked her their first morning here, "I just wanted to apologize for last night, I was mean and spiteful."

"I'm sorry too, I knew what I was getting into. It's not your fault."

"We are both at fault, I did not discourage it." Jason knew she was playing it tough but he also knew she was fragile and had suffered her share of heartbreaks. He honestly was sad that he was the cause of another heartbreak. They sat for a few more minutes but in a more comfortable silence.

"Do you have any plans for today?" he asked her.

"Packing, and I am supposed to go to the Friday night street party with Paul but I have not completely decided about that yet, besides it looks to be a rainy day."

"That was the only thing that Anna was remotely interested in so we may be going."

Molly thought about how she and Jason planned of go as an end of the week celebration. Now that Jason and Anna were going she for sure had little interest in going. And now that she was done with her breakfast she was starting to feel uncomfortable being with an engaged man.

"Jason, I just want to thank you. Not only for this trip but for the hope of the future. You have brought back deeper emotions to my life that I have not felt in a long time. You brought the idea of adventure and travel. The camera has given me a new way to see the world. You did all this Jason. I will forever be grateful and I will never forget this trip or us." She got up and gave him one last soft kiss on his sweet lips and quickly left before he could see the tear run down her cheek.

But he did see and it broke his heart. He jumped up and caught her arm before she made it in the door.

"Molly, I owe it to her to see, we have been together a long time, that is why I am going on to Italy." He almost sounded convincing even to himself.

"I know Jason, I truly hope you find what you are looking for. But remember one thing, the longer you wait the harder it will be to change things. No matter what you do decide."

The storm clouds rolled in and the breeze picked up. It was just as well. Molly did not want to run in to the "couple". She packed up, watched local tv and double checked that she had everything. The storm cleared out just in time to catch one last sunset. Dinner was nice as Paul opted out of the street party as well. She did feel a little bad about that but he understood. They wished each other luck in future relationships and she promised to set up a Facebook account so they could stay in touch. She laughed at that, thinking she would only have two friends but it was a start.

There was no breakfast waiting for her the next morning so she grabbed to go food and coffee for the trip back to the airport, she had already forgotten how bumpy the ride was going up and down the terrain and regretted the coffee she had brought. The rest of the trip was uneventful. When she landed back in New York she was briefly overwhelmed with the crowds and hustle and bustle of the city life. Yet she quickly settled in as it was home, it was what she knew and it was what she was comfortable with.

Chapter 13

Molly had just returned from her ritual Saturday morning coffee with Katie. Katie had not taken the news of how her trip ended very well. She was grateful they all lived and worked in different parts of the city. Jason would have to watch out if Katie ever got near him. For a few weeks Katie was relentless in trying to get Molly to go out but she needed more time. Eventually Katie gave up but only until Molly was done with school. After that Katie threatened to physically drag Molly out of her house if she had to. But Molly did not think that would have to happen, by that time she would be ready.

It was almost Halloween and the air was getting cool and brisk. She was looking forward to cuddling with Coconut. She had gotten a kitten shortly after her trip. It was a rainy evening and as she approached her building she heard little sad meows coming from under a bush. When she looked there was a tiny black and white kitten shivering from being soaking wet. She looked around to see if their was a momma cat or other kittens. There was no way she was going to leave it so she scooped her up and brought her inside. The kitten kept her occupied and she loved her back unconditionally.

Besides finishing school she was truly getting into photography. She learned how to share and edit her photos online thanks to technology and the help of Paul. Paul was a good critic for her. Paul still made her smile, he had asked out another teacher and so far they were still together.

She had settled in on her couch to study for a while before work when someone knocked on her door. Coconut jumped on the floor, excited about the prospect of another person to play with. She did not get a clear picture of who was at the door just by looking through the peephole. She opened the door but only as far as the chain would allow it to go. She stepped back when Jason turned to face her. Jason was the last person she had expected to see and she was at a loss for words. Finally she remembered her manners and invited him in. He still looked good, Molly thought. Well dressed, no doubt thanks to Anna. And he still looked restless both mentally and physically. He walked around her studio not saying much. He focused a lot on her new photos hanging on the wall. There were lot from around the city and a few from their trip including the very first photo taken of them at the airport. It was not a real formal photo but it captured the ease and the free spirit they had together. Jason stared at this photo for a long time.

Jason remembered the day well. As a matter fact memories of the entire trip came flooding back to him. He thought of Molly often but tried hard to keep his memories pushed to the back of his mind. He was also busier than normal these days which helped him stay on track.

Italy was another trip full of shopping. Anna needed outfits as a bride to be, outfits for showers, dress fitting parties and whatever else she said. He lost track. Then when they got home the mothers and the bride were in full planning mode for the wedding which was to be in the spring. Jason got swept up in his job trying to catch up from the two weeks he had off. He was also working longer hours to pay for all the outfits and also to stay out of the planning.

Jason looked around some more taking in the details of the apartment. It was a studio but it was spacious with high ceilings and large windows that looked out onto the tree lined street. The furnishings were minimal with nothing more than she needed. He could see the other souvenirs from their trip hanging on the walls as well. He also noted that the accent colors were the blues and greens of the tropics.

Jason was starting to sweat. He took off his jacket trying to figure out if it was hot in the apartment. He knew it wasn't, that it was the desire starting to build in him again. Desire for Molly, to feel her again and to wrap his body around her. He needed a distraction so he would not let his physical needs take over his body.

"You have become quite the photographer."

"Thanks."

After an awkward silence she asked him what he was doing there.

"I don't know really. I did not have this planned. I missed my stop on the subway. It was like I was in a daze not paying attention to anything. Next thing I know we are past Columbus Circle and of course I'm on the express train so I stayed on."

"You have been taking the subway? That's progress," she smiled at him. There was more awkward silence. Coconut started swatting at his pants which made him jump back. Molly started laughing. "Don't mind Coconut, she is still just a kitten."

Jason bent down to play with her. The kitten was rubbing on his hand then rolling over and swatting at his hands. In typical cat fashion she yawned and walked away when she was done and Jason stood back up rubbing some of the cat hair off his pants. That irritated Molly a little though she knew it shouldn't as they looked like expensive pants. Probably Italian she added to her thoughts.

"Still getting married?" she asked him, but she knew the answer since she had seen the announcement in the social section of the paper. They did not use the photo from St. Lucia, instead it was from Tuscany overlooking the mountains. As a matter of fact her and Katie had gotten a huge laugh out of the whole thing. The announcement had never even mentioned St. Lucia. They had apparently gotten engaged in Tuscany. Anna wanted no record of that trip, she probably would deny ever having been there. Or maybe it was to erase Molly from their history. Either way it seemed just like her and they had managed to laugh over it instead of brooding.

"The announcement said you proposed in Tuscany. Did you?" She was curious if he ever did get down on one knee and ask.

"No, she thought it was just more fitting for us than the Caribbean, she said that was unoriginal. She had no idea what I had planned," he added shoving his hands in his pockets, "but it does not matter now."

"So you never actually asked her then?" She said in slight bewilderment.

"No I guess not." He replied somewhat off guard.

"Interesting. So how are the wedding plans coming?"

"Moving along I guess. Anna is doing most of the planning. I really just have to show up when and where she tells me."

"Hmm," she shrugged her shoulders. Typical of him to let someone else make all the decisions.

"What?" he asked quizzically

"Well it's your wedding too, don't you care about the plans?"

"Sure I guess but it's not really about me."

"Really? You are getting married too, not just her."

Jason started to answer when the phone rang. When she looked at the caller I.D. she went completely white. She had to answer it though. She said nothing except that she understood the situation. Jason was concerned about the sudden change and went over to her to try to figure out what was wrong but she quickly hung up the phone.

"What's wrong?" he asked her with genuine concern.

"I knew that call would come some day just not so soon," she said shaking.

"What call?" he asked. He took her head in his hands to make her look at him. He wanted to keep her attention so she would talk. She was shaking so badly and she was so pale he thought she might pass out.

"He was to only call when she was dead or dying," she managed to say in between shakes.

Jason was quickly trying to remember the who in this when he remembered one of their conversations. "It's your mother."

Molly nodded. "She's in the hospital. She's dying, she wants to see me."

"I will take you." He quickly scanned and found her purse and grabbed her hand to lead her to the door.

"I don't know if I can do this." She stood not moving despite him trying to lead her.

"Molly, listen to me," Jason softened his voice as he turned and stood as close as he could to her without it becoming a full embrace, "I don't want you to ever regret not going, not having that last chance to see and talk to her one more time." He paused to make sure she was still with him, "I will be by your side as much or as little as you want."

Molly just nodded as Jason guided her out the door. She was still pale and shaking even more. He did not even ask her permission to grab a cab. The subway was not an option for him this time. The ride to the hospital was short. Molly was staring straight ahead. He could not even fathom what she was going through. He was glad to be there for her. There had to be some other force involved with this he thought. Or else how did he end up back her place on this day of all days.

When they arrived at the front doors of the hospital he helped Molly out of the cab as she seemed unable or unwilling to move. She was just staring at the doors and now there were tears streaming down her face. He turned and faced her and gently brushed the tears away when he remembered their conversation on the plane.

"Was this where you lost your sister?"

She nodded and buried her face on his chest and sobbed. Jason held her. There was nothing he could say, just give her the time she needed. After a few minutes she took a few deep breaths and stepped back.

"I'm sorry, the memory just came back so strong. The nurses and doctors grabbing her from me and not telling me anything. I was so scared. It was the worst thing I ever experienced and now I have to go see my mother. I have not seen her in so many years. I don't know how I should feel about this."

"Well let's go in and see what the situation is. I think you both will feel at peace if you go ahead and see her."

"Well she better not be expecting anything from me." Molly fought for a long time to get over her anger for her mother, she never quite reached the point of forgiveness though. It eventually just became a part of of her old life that she accepted as fact. She sure was not looking to rehash the past.

Jason just squeezed her hand and let her in the door. They were directed to the intensive care unit. When they reached her bed Jason hung back to give them privacy. Molly was still fighting the memories of her sister being here. If she let them all back she worried that she might faint. There was very little she could focus on that would not bring back some kind of memory. Luckily a nurse approached them and brought her back to the current day and time.

"You must be Molly." The nurse was young and friendly and talked to her in a quiet calming voice. She explained to Molly that her mother had been found on the street passed out. It had not actually been the first time she was there. She knew she had become infected with hepatitis and now she was in complete liver failure and there was nothing left they could do for her. Molly nodded in understanding, although it was only the understanding of what had happened but definitely not with the why she let herself get this way. But she did remember that her mother got hooked so easily on the drugs and probably never had the support or mental strength to get better.

Her mother had a yellow tinge to her skin and eyes. Her eyes were closed and her breaths were slow and erratic. She was always slim but now she was skinny, frail. You could barely see any remnant of the beauty she once was. Molly was still wondering what she should be feeling as no emotion had yet to show. She pulled a chair close to the bed and found her mothers hand. She responded with a deep breath and squeezed back. She opened her sad eyes and looked at Molly.

"I was not sure if you would come. I'm glad you did."

Molly just smiled at her and reached over to push her sweat soaked hair away from her face. It must be an old instinct to take care of her in some small way. Her mother smiled and closed her eyes again. She took a few more deep breaths and looked back at her daughter.

"You deserved better. You and your sister." She was straining with each word and breath. "I never regretted either one of you."

She struggled for a few more breaths. She gave Molly a folded piece of paper. "Call them, they are your family." Now she was really struggling. She had a tight grip on Molly's hand. Molly felt she needed to say something that would ease her mind.

"It's ok, go now and be with Julie."

Her mother took took two more breaths, gasped and Molly felt the grasp on her hand ease up. Her EKG flat lined. Molly took one last look, grabbed the folded paper and walked away. She wanted to be out of the room before the nurses and doctors rushed in, she did not want to be asked any questions and she did not want to sign anything. She found Jason in the waiting area.

"Let's go," she said and walked back to the elevators.

"How is your mother?" he asked scurrying to catch up.

"She is gone," she replied matter of fact.

"Were you able to talk to her?" He needed to at least know that she could have some closure. Molly nodded as her only response. But with this he also realized that the two people closest to her had basically died in her arms. He could not imagine how she was feeling. She was showing more anger than anything else. He followed her as she walked quickly back to the elevators. He decided silence would be better and she would talk when she was ready, but that took a while as she said nothing all the way back to her apartment. She did not protest another cab ride or the fact that he went inside with her.

Molly went over to her window and stared out. Finally she started talking quietly so that Jason had to stand near her.

"Do you know what the worst thing of all this is?" she turned and faced him. "That she gets to be with

Julie. What did she ever do for her? And now she gets to see her. She did not say she loved us just that she never regretted us." Molly was almost laughing now. "What does that mean? That we were not quite the burden I thought we were?"

Jason moved towards her, his heart breaking for her. He knew she was avoiding the true emotion and that somewhere inside she was grieving. It was still the mother she had spent much of her life with, good or bad, so it had to hurt to lose her. He put his arms around her to try to comfort her. He also wanted to give her a signal that she could relax but it had the opposite effect as Molly started yelling at him.

"Don't start that now. You somehow manage to show up on this day and now you think you can comfort me. You just left me, never even asked if I got home okay. And how do you think I feel every time your picture shows up in the social pages? You are just like everyone else in my life. You win my heart and my trust then you break it and leave." Molly knew that was not entirely fair but he led her on as well and then nothing.

"Just leave Jason."

That was a slap in the face for him but she was right. He wanted to talk to her when he got back but the longer he waited the harder it was to pick up the phone and then it was just easier to let it go. He turned to go but looked back at her "I'm sorry for everything," then he left her again.

And just like before that was when she was able to break down and let her tears flow. Her true mother, the one that was full of life and energy had died a long time ago but now there was nothing. She looked down at the piece of paper. She stared at it for a long time until she realized someone was knocking at the door again, it better not be Jason she thought, he was the last person she wanted to see. But it was not, it was Katie. She opened the door to let her in and held on to the one person that never left her and never let her down.

"Oh honey, I am so sorry. I was in shock to get a text from Jason, I forgot we exchanged numbers at the airport. You were on your way home from the hospital when he sent it and then I called to see what happened with your mother."

"Katie, it was awful. She looked terrible. I could not think of anything to say. I guess she said her peace because she died right after." She cried some more while Katie just held on to her. "She gave me a number to call. It must be my grandparents."

Katie stepped back and covered her mouth in amazement. "Are you going to call them, I can't believe she kept them from you all this time."

"You can't believe it? I will probably give some little old lady a heart attack. Besides this phone number can't still be good can it?"

"Well, there is only one way to find out."

Molly sat down contemplating what she should do. She wondered why her mother had kept her grandparents, her only relatives from her all this time. Maybe she was too embarrassed to get in touch with them. Parents are forgiving though and always want to help their kids especially grandkids. So why not now, would they still feel the same way or would they want nothing to do with her? It did not really matter she supposed as she lived without them all these years but could she handle another rejection?

"What if I cause them too much pain and they won't have anything to do with me?"

"Look, you can only gain by this, you can't lose what you don't have so let them decide and if they can't handle it then you still have me and momma and papa."

"I love you Katie," Molly said hugging Katie.

"You too honey, I have to get back to work, call me," she hugged her back and hurried out the door.

Molly was left alone again. She thought of who else she call to ask for advice. She already knew Katie's mom would just tell her to call. Instead she dialed her old superintendents number but got no answers. He did not recall her grandparents ever coming by or anyone looking for her or her mother except her fathers supposed acquaintances. It would be nice to have family of her own, she could invite them to her graduation and they would tell her how proud they were. She smiled at that thought, no one outside of Katie's family ever told her that except Jason. She sighed, one way or another her life would go on like always.

She decided to call them and let them make the decision unless of course they were totally creepy or weird or criminals. She had not thought that the reason her mother left home was because of her parents. Maybe she could check a criminal history on them. No, that was crazy she thought, she knew she was just procrastinating and needed to just dial the number. She took a deep breath and with shaking hands punched the numbers into her phone.

Chapter 13

She had already decided that she would not leave a message, it seemed worse to hear what she had to say on voicemail. She actually hoped they would answer so she would not have to contemplate calling again. She almost hung up when on the sixth ring a woman answered.

"Hello," the woman said cheerfully but slightly out of breath.

Molly was also breathing hard and almost did not answer when the woman said hello again and asked if there was anyone there.

Molly found her voice although that too was a little shaky. "Oh I'm sorry, I am looking for Mrs. Mary Conner."

"This is her, who is calling?" Mary responded with caution, probably expecting another sales call.

"My name is Molly, you don't know me. Do you have a daughter named Susan?" Molly had to sit down she was so nervous, she hoped Mary was sitting down as well.

"Yes," she said cautiously, "but I have not heard from her in a long time. Who did you say you were again?" now Mary was the one that was starting to shake, Molly could hear it in her voice.

"My name is Molly," she hesitated then added, "I am Susan's daughter." There was a thud and then silence, Molly was pretty sure that Mary had dropped the phone.

"Who is this?" a man came on sounding rather angry.

"I am sorry sir, but I believe I am your granddaughter. My name is Molly and my mother is Susan Conner."

"How did you get this number?"

"My mother gave it to me today."

"I see."

"You do?" That was it? That was all he had to say? In her head she knew this must be a shock but her heart was aching in so many ways and she was angry.

"Because I don't. My mother kept it from me for a long time. Do you know why? Is there something wrong with you guys?"

"No of course not," he said a little gruff. He took a moment then continued calmly, "I don't know why she did that, well maybe I do but it's a long story. How is she by the way?"

"She died today," Molly said matter of fact as there was no other way to say it. She felt bad for them, springing this on them out of the blue but they had a right to know just like she did. Maybe once they were over the shock they could have a more productive conversation.

"Listen, I know this must be a shock and I don't expect anything from you or your wife but I just thought you should know."

"Absolutely, thank you for the call." Molly thought that was the end of it when Mary came back on the phone and said, "wait, how is Susan?"

"I'm sorry ma'am I just told your husband that she passed away today. Look it's okay if this is too much I'll just go now." Molly was feeling really bad to the point of regretting the call but Mary kept her on the line.

"No please don't go. It's just so unexpected, you must understand that. Please I want to meet you. When can we do that, where do you live?"

"I live in the city but I have no car so if it is okay you can come here."

"Yes anytime we can leave in an hour."

"I'm sorry I have had a rough day as well if it is okay we can make it tomorrow evening, I can make us dinner."

"Yes of course we are looking forward to it."

They exchanged numbers and addresses and hung up. Molly felt a huge relief but she was still somewhat nervous about the whole thing. She hoped they could tell her why they had not spoken to her mother in so long. But she was also interested in her mothers childhood, she had not talked about it very much only to say that it was pretty normal. Molly was also pretty hopeful at the thought of having a family again. She called Katie and filled her in. She went to bed and dreamed of having Mary and Sean at her graduation and maybe even at her wedding someday.

The next morning Molly was awakened by a knocking at the door again. She was not ready to talk to anyone just yet. After the emotional roller coaster of yesterday she had planned on staying in bed a little later. The knocking would not stop so she took the pillow off her head and yelled for the intruder to go away.

"Delivery," was the muffled response.

Molly got up and peeked through the door and saw a delivery man with a bakery box in his hand. She grabbed a few singles from her purse and opened the door.

"I did not order anything."

"Molly Delgado?"

"Yes."

"This is for you," he shoved the box at her and she gave him a tip which he took without looking and quickly left.

Molly took the box to her table that doubled for dining and school work. She cleared her books and set the box down. There were two smaller boxes inside, one cardboard, one plastic. She opened the smaller box to find an assortment of fruit including raspberries, blackberries, strawberries and pineapple. Molly started munching on the berries and opened the second larger box to find several pastries. It was the same breakfast Jason would leave for her on her patio. She looked in the box for a card or note but there was none. She knew that it could only be from Jason though, it was just like the breakfast they used to share watching the new days sunlight spread out over the ocean. She wished he had included a note, some words so she could figure out what he was thinking. She felt for sure they still had a connection and she could feel his confusion he had when he had showed up at her door. She sighed, there was nothing she could do, she was still determined that he had to make his own choices and ultimately they would both have to live with it.

Molly spent the rest of the day cleaning and preparing dinner. She made a lasagna as it occupied her day and then she could just heat it up. It was sure to be an emotional evening and she would not be able to trust her self not to break down emotionally once her grandparents got here. Grandparents, that word stuck on her head, she could not believe she was meeting blood relatives. She often dreamed as a child what it would be like to have grandparents that would buy her little things and take her places or that her and Julie might spend the weekend with them. She had learned quickly to stop asking about them. Obviously there had been a huge falling out between them, maybe she could discover why today. No matter what happened in the past she wanted a fresh start with this relationship and she would make her own judgements.

Right at six o' clock her door bell rang. Molly was so nervous and she was sure they would be as well. She took a deep breath and opened the door. No one moved, the three just stood there taking each one in. Molly could see her mother in both of them. Mary had red hair although she suspected it was dyed as Sean had silver hair. They were both tall and slim. They looked athletic and active on what passed for a tan for people of Irish descent. Mary had tears in her eyes and she was trembling. She brought her hand to her mouth and started forward. She wrapped her arms around Molly. Molly stiffened slightly, not used to the physical touch of strangers but then she relaxed and gave her grandmother a hug back. Eventually she managed to break free just long enough to let the pair into her apartment. She gave Sean a hug as well as he passed though the door.

There was still an awkward silence as they came in and had a quick look around. Molly was not sure how to start the conversation so she started with something simple.

"So any problems getting here?"

"No we actually came in a little early and took a walk around, did some window shopping. Then we came up this way so we would have an easier time finding parking and strolled around the park," her grandfather was a little nervous too as he was rambling a little talking about the traffic and which route and bridge to take.

Molly asked if they came to city often, wanting to know how close they had been to each other all these years.

"Not as often as we used to," was the only response Sean offered

Molly brought out bottles of wine, she was not sure which they preferred so she got red, white and rose.

They each poured a glass and took a sip. It seemed to help everyone relax a bit. Molly directed everyone over to the couch. Her grandmother started to well up again.

"I'm sorry, except for the dark hair, you look just like your mother. What was your fathers background?"

"He was one hundred percent Italian."

"Do you keep in touch with him?"

"No I have not seen him since I was six I think." Molly had few memories of him and none of them were good.

Mary was starting to tremble again so she took another sip of her wine, she took Molly's hand and looked at her, "how did Susan die?"

Molly knew that she would have to answer some difficult questions, she dreaded it but better to let it all out now. "She died of hepatitis, she was drug and alcohol addicted and went into acute liver failure. There was nothing they could really do for her."

Mary and Sean just nodded in silence. Molly knew they were mourning for her all over again. They had already lost her once when she chose not to talk to them but maybe they never gave up hope and now they had to face the reality they would never see her again. Molly needed to know what happened.

"I know this is hard but what happened, why did you stop seeing each other?"

Mary was silently sobbing so Sean jumped in. "Your mother was talented. She wanted to be a Broadway star. She always had the leading roles in her high school plays. She could sing and dance. She even did some local theater. She was ready to take on the world. Make in big in New York."

Mary took a big breath to ease her sobs and continued with the story. "We tried to convince her to go to college, study drama some more and continue to do plays and get more experience. We had the money, we were going to pay for it. She filled out a few applications to appease us but ultimately she decided not to go and since she was eighteen we could not make her. So we helped her out any way we could. We made the initial rent payments, sent her money for food. We talked often and visited her. She claimed to have gotten some parts in up and coming plays. But we knew better. She stopped answering our calls and would not let us see her. She said she was fine though, making her rent by waitressing. One day she called and was so happy, she had landed a part in a new play. Maybe that was so but the play never took off."

Mary was becoming distressed from the memories so Sean took back over. "We think she was embarrassed initially then we thought maybe she had gotten into trouble or met the wrong people. One day we went to see her. She was there but obviously high on something. We wanted to bring her home right then. She started screaming at us to leave her alone, that she was on the brink of fame. She met someone who promised her a big break. So we left. That was our mistake since when we went back the next day she was gone." Sean started to tremble now and his eyes were glassy. "It was our mistake to leave her that day." He repeated.

Molly felt really bad for them. "It would not have mattered. You must know that. She would have left again."

Mary responded to that. "We know and have come to accept it. But it is hard when it is your own child. You will never feel like you did enough."

Molly got up to put the lasagna in the oven. She needed a little space. She knew her turn was next. They would want to hear the rest of the story of her mothers life. It would not be easy to tell. It was okay when she told Jason. It was like a weight lifted off her shoulders. But for her grandparents it would just be more heartbreak.

When she went back to the couch Mary asked if they saw each other often.

"I have not seen her in nine years." Molly stated starting to feel anxious.

"What happened?"

Molly took a deep breath and rubbed her hands. "I was very angry at her," was all she could manage. The memories were coming back to her again. She was hoping this was the last time she had to visit this part of her past.

"Please tell us what happened," Mary softly pleaded.

Molly turned on the couch to face them and put her legs up while she hugged her kitty in one arm. She took her grandmothers hand with her other hand. It was warm and soothing just as she dreamt it would be. It gave her the courage to tell the story one last time.

"I had a sister named Julie. She died when she was eight and I blamed my mother." This started a new round of tears from everyone including Sean this time. Molly kept going though. She picked up where they left off. Telling them of the people her mother had actually met and how she got pregnant. She told them about Julie's health problems and how her father had left them. She wanted them to know Julie was her life and those were her happy days. She briefly explained what happened they day she died. It was too much for her to tell again and knew it would be too much for them to hear. They did not need to know it, she planned on telling them all the fun things they did together anyway. That is how she wants them to think of Julie.

"So I was angry. I never forgave her. Her depression and addictions got worse. So I went to work and when I was able to afford the rent I kicked her out. I have been on my own ever since."

Mary leaned over and wrapped her arms around her granddaughter, they both let the tears silently stream down their faces. She pulled back and looked at Molly. "We tried to find her. Please know we tried."

Molly nodded in understanding. "You could not find her because she took my fathers name. I only found out from my old landlord they never legally married."

Sean nodded back, "there was no paper trail to follow. We always looked though. Even right up to you calling us. Somehow we always hoped we would open the entertainment section and see her there. We were able to move on with life after a long time and with the help of friends. There was nothing left to do. There was always a missing person report on file. She did not want to be found and ultimately we knew it."

Molly got up to set the dinner table. They needed a break and she hoped to turn the conversation to a more cheery topic. She showed them the bathroom so they could freshen up. They met back up at the dinner table and refreshed their drinks and filled their plates.

Molly smiled, "I hope you like Italian."

"It looks wonderful, where did you learn to cook?" Mary asked.

"Cooking shows," Molly responded, "I got tired of microwave dinners."

Molly saw Mary bite her lips. She looked upset that she had not grown up with home cooked meals. Molly was ready to let the past go and move on just as they had and now they could do it again together.

"I just want you to know I did not have a horrible life. I always had food, clothes and a roof over my head. We never moved and I had a sister who loved me and I had someone to care for. My life now is good. I work hard and I am graduating college in two months. I am happy. I want to get to know both of you and be a family. But I want to be able to do it without thinking of the past or thinking of the what ifs and what could have been. I learned a long time ago to accept life and make it my own. No one was going to do it for me. I work hard to get the things I have. I want you in my life but only going forward and only with happy memories."

Mary promised that her tears would be the last and she agreed to only talk about good times. They spent the rest of the evening sharing those good memories. Susan had an idyllic childhood with lots of friends and sleepovers and birthday parties. She took dance and singing lessons and they went on family trips every summer. Molly shared stories of her time with Julie and how they spent their days at the park and how they were ghosts every Halloween. They talked about her schooling and she invited them to her graduation. She was so excited at the prospect of having actual family there. She told them about Katie and her family. They were all going to the graduation as well. They asked her about boyfriends.

"Much to Katie's disapproval," Molly said laughing, "I have spent too much time working and studying. That is all I have done for a long time. I always planned for my life to start when I graduated. That is what I always told her. Well perhaps I missed out on some things but it was worth it I think." Her grandparents gave her a look of slight confusion.

"I met someone over the summer. It was such a random meeting. We got to know each other and we took a trip together."

"So what happened?"

Molly smiled and pronounced that he was engaged. "Don't worry I knew it, I jumped in to his arms anyway and in the end I guess it was not meant to be."

"But you don't believe that do you?"

Molly looked at Mary in wonderment, did grandmothers just have a sense to read people? She was not sure how she would know what she was feeling about Jason. Maybe it was a family thing after all.

"Jason treated me like I was the only woman on earth when we were together. He listened to me, respected me and made me feel special. We had fun together too but when he was around his girlfriend, fiancé soon to be wife he was like a robot. Whatever she told him to do he would." Laughing Molly added, "he had this romantic trip planned for them but she did not want to go so he offered for me to go instead. He was trying to make her jealous but she never saw me as a threat so she agreed with his offer thinking he would never do it so I took them up on it and went. He was so free and relaxed without her. Okay, I know I am rambling on, anyway, I guess just like you I still have hope that he will come back."

"He is a fool if he does not," Sean said.

Dinner tuned into dessert and it was getting late and they were all tired and emotionally spent. Mary and Sean got up and they gave each other long meaningful hugs. Molly asked them to spend Thanksgiving with her and Katie's family. They promised to visit on the weekends and come for her graduation. Molly saw them out after one more hug. She looked through her peep hole and just as she suspected Mary was sobbing in Sean's arms. Hopefully their mourning would be easier this time and a new happier relationship would take its place. Molly knew that was true for her. There were new people in her life that loved her unconditionally and that was enough for her.

Chapter 14

Molly was overwhelmed with emotions. Sitting in the auditorium, she was excited, elated and relieved as well. This was the moment she had been waiting for since she started saving her hard earned money. She dreamed of this for a long time, wearing the black cap and gown and gold honor cords. She was only half listening to the speeches. She knew all about hard work and the rewards and how to grab life's opportunities and take them. She did not need to listen to a twenty one year old tell her how to live her life to the fullest. Maybe she had not quite done that yet but she had plans. She had already spent time with her grandparents and they joined her and Katie's family for Thanksgiving. Molly had traveled to their house to see them as well. She had not yet thought about Christmas. She had spent many of them with Katie but still wanted to include her grandparents. She would work it out.

The nice thing about graduation in December was the smaller ceremony. She would actually hear her name called to pick up her diploma. There would be hooting and hollering as all of Katie's family was here for her including her loud brothers. But they were all proud of her and she could not wait to hear them.

She stood up with her row to head towards the stage. Molly was trying to savor every moment. From the sea of black gowns to the excitement and hope for the future. She was next to go and stopped at the bottoms of the stairs. She took a deep breath and closed her eyes. When they called her name her heart beat faster and all her nerves tingled. Then she heard the cheers from her family and she smiled. This was her moment, she climbed the stairs and walked toward the Dean of Education. Her smile grew bigger and bigger. She took her diploma cover, shook the Dean's hand and smiled out towards her family. They were out there somewhere even if she could not see them. She hugged her reward and walked off the other side of the stage back to her seat. A tear of joy slid down her cheek.

After the ceremony they all went out to eat at an Italian restaurant. The conversation was lively, the wine was flowing and everyone was having a great time. Katie's family had accepted not just her but her grandparents as family as well. Molly smiled to herself. Life was so good right now. She was looking forward to some new free time and preparing to have her own classroom the next school year.

Katie jolted her thoughts when she asked to see her diploma. "Oh it's just a cover, they will mail the real one to me. They have to make sure we passed our classes and met all of our requirements."

"I know I just want to see."

"Okay," Molly replied slowly and handed it over.

"Hey did you look inside, there is something in here."

"What, is it a note saying your diploma goes here, like we could not figure that out after all that college education?" Molly replied with a chuckle.

"Ha, ha, look see what it is."

Molly took the cover with reluctance. She opened it to see a handwritten note. It said congratulations. Please meet me for breakfast tomorrow at 9 am at your favorite diner. Molly was confused. This had also caught everyone's attention, the conversations stopped and everyone was looking at her.

"How did this get in here, and how do I know this is even for me? There was a huge stack of these with no names attached. It could have been for anyone." Then Molly had a sudden thought and looked at Katie when she said, "or you put it in here, tell me who is it from?"

Katie looked at her with one of those I don't know what you are talking about looks. "It was not me, I don't know who it was from."

Molly looked at each person in turn and each person gave her a shrug of their shoulders. "Well it must not be for me then," she decided and crumpled up the note.

Katie was still nonchalant but replied with, "well you will never know if you don't go."

Molly was hoping that by crumpling the note someone would break down and clue her in. They either did not know or they were good actors. She had never known Katie to be able to keep a secret from her. That is why this was so confusing. Katie was really convincing right now but it was also strange that she being quiet about it. She would have expected her to speculate about who it could be from or how it would have gotten there. She did not open it early knowing there would be nothing interesting in it so she had no way of knowing when it had gotten there. Well there was no use over thinking this, obviously no one was talking or they did not know either.

"Well I guess I have nothing to lose. I will go and see if I know anyone and if not I will have breakfast."

Molly looked over at Katie. She seemed truly immersed in her dinner and would not look up but she had a small grin that told Molly she knew what was going on. Molly let it go since Katie was trying so hard to keep quiet.

Dinner was over and the party broke up with promises of getting together soon. Katie gave her a great big hug and made her promise that she had to come out more and meet more people. Molly agreed as that was on her start her new life list. Her grandparents lingered behind.

Mary said to Molly, "we are so proud of everything you accomplished. We saved for a long time in the hopes of sending your mother to college. We never spent the money. We were hoping the right moment would come when we could decide what to do with it. We want you to have it. To do whatever you need, pay for student loans, take some time off, go on vacation. Whatever you need."

Sean handed Molly an envelope. Molly could not believe it. She suddenly remembered her wish on the beach and how she told Jason she wanted to be able to pay for some one else's college education some day. She opened the card and read the heartfelt words of congratulations. She slowly turned the check over and her jaw dropped. It was way more money than than she could have dreamed. She suddenly thought of all the things that she could do. All of the things Mary mentioned and pay for someone to get a head start in life. But she hesitated.

"I can't possibly take this. This is way too much. Besides between work and scholarships I don't have any student loans."

Sean was truly impressed and more proud then ever. "The money has been accumulating interest for a long time. When the economy went bad we lost some but moved it to a safe account. It was supposed to be for Susan so consider it your reward, your inheritance, whatever but it is for you. We have what we need and you are just getting started. We will not take no for an answer."

Molly's hands were shaking and she could feel the tears well up. She always counted on herself and rewarded herself. This was beyond her little wish on a star.

"I promise to use it wisely. Someday I will give someone a scholarship and pay for their education."

"We know you are responsible. Please promise us that you will do something for yourself."

"Oh I will, thank you so much." Molly hugged them both. She closed her eyes and soaked in the love. Despite all the turmoil of her life she had silently thanked her mother for reuniting her with her grandparents.

Back at her apartment while she was playing with her kitty she thought about the events of the and even the past few months. She would be able to pay off her last bill. She was going to give her notice at the supermarket. She would take Christmas week off with the rest of the school and not work any other job. She could not remember the last time so had no school, no homework to squeeze in between jobs. But then she remembered her trip to St. Lucia which brought her back to the note left in her diploma cover. Could it have somehow been from him? She did not see how he could have someone slip it in there. She doubted Katie would even give him the time of day. Maybe she had a secret admirer from one her classes. She thought of who it might be but she never paid much attention to anyone else. Then she thought of who she wanted it to be. Jason caused her too much emotional turmoil. If he just wanted to congratulate her then talk about Anna he could have just sent her a card. Maybe it would be better if it really was not for her. Then she remembered Katie's grin. She had to trust her friend. Katie has only ever wanted her to be happy.

Chapter 15

Molly felt peaceful when she awoke the next morning. The light was just making its way through her curtains and she knew there would not be any more sleep for her. While it was not the most deep sleep she ever had she felt that no matter what happened this morning the rest of her life was where she always dreamed it would be. She got out of bed and looked out the window and saw a grey sky but it was the kind of grey that held the promise of snow. The trees were still which meant the air was cool but there would be no wind seeping through your clothes. Since it was still a little early Molly decided on a hot bath to warm her bones and relax her mind. She found her mind wandering back to her trip to St. Lucia, but it was more to feel the warm sun and smell the tropical sea air. Then she thought of where her next travels would take her. Maybe a weekend trip to the nations capital would be a good way to start solo traveling or she should just go all out and go big. Perhaps she could treat Katie to a girls weekend.

Oh well, plenty of time to decide. After a quick hair washing she got out and dressed. She decided to go practical since it was cold outside. She had not had the chance to completely update her wardrobe. Still she felt pretty good in the jeans and sweater she chose. She added her coat, scarf and mittens and headed out the door.

The air was cool and crisp just as Molly thought. Since there was no wind the day was bearable. She could see her breath as she walked and was glad she chose warm and practical clothing. For all she knew there would be no one to impress anyway. She would know soon enough. As she walked the few blocks to the cafe she debated on peeking in the window first but ultimately there were too many people blocking her view.

She pushed though the morning crowd scanning the tables. She continued looking but did not see anyone she recognized. Molly had mixed feelings over that. Relief and disappointment crossed her mind at the same time. But maybe her mystery date was not there yet, she started to turn to head back to the door when she heard a newspaper rustle. The noise caught her attention and she turned to look. Her body started to tingle starting at her fingertips and running down to her toes. It was him but not him at the same time. Jason was there. This was the Jason Molly knew from St. Lucia. She knew just by the way his hair was ruffled and his change in clothing style. Her heart leapt and it gave her hope but she was still cautious as this still could be another send off, good bye and good luck, have a nice life. She hoped it was not, she could not handle that again.

Molly walked to the table on slightly unsteady legs but took a deep breath to calm her nerves. "Hi Jason," she stared straight into his eyes as she slid in the booth opposite of him. It took him a minute to respond and a surge of fear went through her as she thought briefly that maybe he was not here for her. Then he smiled at her and she immediately felt relief. She missed his smile and how the world seemed right when she was with him.

She could tell that he was nervous though as he fiddled with his coffee cup.

"Hi Molly, you look great."

"Thanks. You look good too, I like your haircut and the jacket suits you." His hair was less then perfect and he was wearing a black leather jacket. It appeared to have a hood but when she looked closer it was the hood of the Baja she had given him. She smiled inwardly.

Another awkward silence. Molly picked up the menu even though she knew everything that was on it. She wished he would start talking first.

"I hope you don't mind I took the liberty of ordering for us." Molly put her menu back and unwrapped her silverware and fiddled with her fork. She wanted to know if he was getting married but was also scared of the answer so she switched her train of thought.

"Neat trick, getting the note into my diploma cover."

Jason grinned and seemed to relax slightly. "I had a little help."

"Must have been a big big bribe to get Katie to help you. I am surprised you have no broken bones."

"It took some convincing," Molly raised her eyebrow at that, "okay a lot of convincing, including a threat to have her brothers after me. Your friend can be a little scary."

"She's a good friend."

"Well I wanted to personally congratulate you on your diploma. It's an amazing accomplishment."

"Thanks," she replied with a tentative smile, wondering if this was the only reason he was here.

The food arrived. It was her favorite, a plate of pancakes, since the diner did not have a variety of pastries, and fresh fruit. She smiled and remembered their sunrise breakfasts. She had been trying to not reminisce as often hoping it would eventually just be a good memory. But the hurt would still come through on occasion. She had to know what his status was.

"So how are things with you?" She asked him

He nodded as he had a mouth full of eggs. He wiped is mouth and managed to get out one word. "Good."

"How are the wedding plans coming, it's in the spring right?"

He could tell she was holding her breath. He wanted to tell her as soon as she walked in the door but he was afraid she would reject him. He wanted to get a sense of how she was feeling especially towards him. She was not giving much away though. She seemed as nervous as he was. He was still trying to get over the fact that she was even here and talking to him. He really did not deserve another chance with her but he had to try and he was not going to give up without a fight,

"I'm not getting married," he stated as he stared into her eyes waiting for her reaction.

"Hmm," was all she could say and then she started eating bite after bite.

Not the reaction he expected or hoped for. His heart sank a little but he had to keep trying. "After I saw you last and seeing what you went through with your mother I did some soul searching. I thought a lot about what I wanted. Not what everyone expected me to do. I thought about where I wanted to be in life." He paused and took her hands is his. "And who I wanted to be with."

Molly dropped her fork and bit her lip. She actually clamped her hands into a fist when he took them. She was trying hard not to shake. When he started rubbing his thumbs across the top of her hands she finally started to relax and softened her grip. She looked back into his eyes and saw the familiar look. The one that told her he only saw her and not anyone or anything else. The one that made her feel like she did matter.

He kept holding her hands and kept his gaze in her eyes. "I realized that everything I had and did was decided by someone else. My college, my job, my apartment, furniture and my clothes as you once pointed out to me."

That got a chuckle out of both of them.

"But what about Anna, no one picked her for you."

"No but we ran in the same circles, with our friends and family. Our relationship was good for a while. But then we were just together. So we stayed together and then it seemed like the next step was to get engaged so we did. You took control of your life, controlled your destiny. That is what I needed to do."

She quietly asked, "so what did you find out on your soul searching?"

"I realized I hated my clothes. I did not like my apartment or the furnishings."

"What about your job?"

"I actually do like my job and it has been good to me allowing me financial freedom but I have plans to start new programs. I want to reach out to lower income families and even high school students to teach them that even small investments can make a difference."

"So you kept your job, changed your clothes, nice Baja by the way, what else?"

He smiled at that and took his leather jacket off, he was glad she noticed. "I sold my apartment with everything in it. Except for work clothes and a few other things from our trip. I packed a duffle bag and handed the keys over."

"So where are you living now?"

"No where really, I spend a lot time at my office or I crash at my parents house."

"How do they feel about all of this."

"They support my decision."

"I can't believe you sold all your things."

"I did not pick them so I am not sure if I really liked any of it."

Molly could not decide if that was brave or stupid. After working so hard to to get her home she could not imagine letting it go so easily. Then again it was easier when you had the money. They had both finished their breakfast and she was ready to get out of the stuffy diner.

"Do you want to go for a walk? The park is not quite as colorful but it is quiet this time of year."

"Sure, but I want to give you something before we leave."

She watched him pull out a wrapped box. It looked to be a shirt sized box but she could not imagine what he would have bought for her.

"That is really nice of you, you have given me so much already." She did mean it but she was getting used to getting a few gifts now and then and she was enjoying it. She took off the wrapping paper and set the box down on the table. She lifted the top off to find a framed certificate. It seemed that Jason bought her a star and had it named after Julie. She sat stunned for a few moments as she ran her finger across Julie's name.

She rewarded Jason with a huge grin, "do you think we can see her star at night?"

He hoped she would not be disappointed, "probably not, I think it is pretty far away."

"That's okay, I will think about every time I see the stars at night. I love this, it really means a lot to me."

And once again he knew just what was important to her.

Jason took the frame to put back in his backpack, they got up from the table and he paid the bill. He was feeling more relaxed. He was happy with how things were going but he was still afraid he would screw this up. He felt he should be saying more but did not want to scare her off or move too fast. He still needed more time to assess how she felt about him so he was thrilled to spend more time with her.

They bundled up and headed out the door. A blast of cold air hit them both. Jason instinctively wrapped his arm around Molly's shoulder. Even though she had multiple layers on it warmed her from the inside to feel him that close again. She snuggled into him as they headed towards the park entrance,

"Subway or cab?"

He smiled and said, "subway, the people watching is great."

As they entered the park there was a swirl of wind and the leaves formed a little tornado around them. Then a few snowflakes started to fall. Jason drew Molly in even closer as they continued down the path. Molly did not want him to let go. It was too heart breaking the first time. She had to make a decision. Let him back in again and trust him or let him go forever this time She started to shiver but not from being cold even though the snowflakes were getting fatter and wetter. The branches were quickly turning into white arms reaching out to them.

Jason stopped her and turned to face her. The snowflakes were falling faster dusting Molly's hair in a white halo. She looked beautiful. Her eyes were glistening and her cheeks were rosy pink.

"Are you cold, do you want to turn back?"

"No I'm okay." But she was scared still and she looked down fighting back tears. The emotions of the last few months and days starting to overwhelm her.

Jason saw her sudden distress and hoped he could make it right knowing that he was likely the cause.

"What's wrong?" He tilted her head up so he could look into her eyes again.

She asked him the same question she just a few weeks ago, "Jason why are you here?"

"I needed to see you again, I have never stopped thinking of you. I needed to see that you are okay. Every time I write something at work, I think of you." He spoke the words with confidence but they were not quite the words she wanted to hear.

"Is that all? Because I can not keep seeing you every once in a while." She turned away from him, still trying to fight back tears.

Jason's heart sank, she did not want to see him but maybe she did not understand, he obviously was not good at expressing his feelings all the time. He had not said the words he was about to say to her yet but he felt it all through his mind and body.

"Molly, I am here because I love you, with all my heart. I am here because I want to be with you and no one else. I have been wandering aimlessly this last week, these last few months really. I am homeless because I want to be with you. I can't imagine anything or anyone else." He paused and turned to face her again. The tears were streaming down her face. Maybe he was too late and already ruined it. "Unless you can't let me back in your life. And if that is the case I understand and I will let you go."

Molly looked up into Jason's eyes and saw the sincerity, the love he was sending her way. She realized that he was it. There was no more looking and decided to take this last chance. She slid down on her knees and took his hands into hers.

"Jason, I have been in love with you since you walked onto my register line. I can not imagine my life without you. I don't let too many people in my life but the ones I have are amazing. You are one of the amazing people. I can't risk losing any one of them. I want you more than anything Jason. I want to be with you all the time. Jason come home with me, stay with me." Molly took once last deep breath and squeezed his hands even harder. "Jason marry me, promise to be with me forever."

Jason stood in shock for a moment. That was supposed to be his question to her. It had been in the back of his mind the whole morning and she beat him to it. He smiled, it must be fate, she was truly his soulmate.

When he did not respond right away she let go of his hands and sat back on her feet. This snapped him out of his thoughts and he kneeled down in front of her. He leaned forward and took her head in his hands. He wiped the snow off her eyelashes, leaned forward and kissed her beautiful lips. Oh how he missed her soft lips. He started with a soft sweeping across her lips then he deepened his kiss. They kissed with such passion and created so much heat they could have melted the snow all around them. When they came up for air they were both breathing hard. Jason reached into the inside pocket of his leather coat and pulled out a small rectangular box.

Molly was still coming up for air and her head was dizzy when she saw the box. He opened it and there was the most beautiful diamond ring she ever saw. It was diamond shape flanked by smaller diamonds. Her tears started flowing again. She could not believe they had the same thoughts but she stilled loved that she asked first and she loved him. He slid the ring on her finger and it fit perfectly.

"Not only will I marry you, but I promise to make my own decision, most of the time," he chuckled.

She wrapped her arms around him, "let's go home Jason." He scooped her up in his arms and started carrying her back.

She thought about her home and while it suited her she did not think it would suit both of them very long. "I would like to find a new home. Something a little bigger maybe?"

"Something we can pick together," he added.

She snuggled her head on his shoulder, all of her wishes came true. She smiled up at the sky and winked at Julie.

About the Author

I have been an avid reader all of my life. I read most genres including historical novels, action and thriller and contemporary romance novels. I also have a large collection of Star Wars novels. I started writing as a hobby. I fell in love with my characters and I wanted to share them with the world. I want to continue creating characters and stories that draw from my life experiences.

I have been working in the veterinary field for the last fourteen years, four years as an assistant and ten years as a Licensed Veteunary Technicin. Animals have become important members of families and I enjoy taking care of them. I currently live with two dogs, two cats, a rabbit and a buch of fish. We also keep a horse not to far from our house.

When I am not being a devoted wife and mother of two girls, I take tap and jazz classes, ride ponies and I am the treasurer of my daughters pony club. I also love to travel, draw, and take photographs.